McCracken
and the
Lost Lady

We emerged from the canal and into Venice's open lagoon, the launch bouncing over the wave-tops. Ahead of us lay a small island, on which rose a crumbling old mansion that must once have belonged to a wealthy Italian merchant. The sun was beginning to set, and I could see that a single light burned in one of the windows.

We moored our boat at a little jetty, and climbed some rickety steps to a small courtyard, then entered the house. I found myself in a wide hallway with sweeping stairs at one end and doors to left and right. Hat nodded towards the right-hand door, and I walked through it into a room that was furnished with a table, a few chairs, and a solid sideboard that looked as if it were about four hundred years old.

A long time seemed to pass, before the door opened and a man entered. He wasn't who I expected, but I recognized him at once, of course.

"Your Holiness!" I cried, and falling to my knees before him, I kissed the Fisherman's Ring.

Also by Mark Adderley

The Hawk and the Wolf
The Hawk and the Cup
The Hawk and the Huntress

For Young Readers:
McCracken and the Lost Island
McCracken and the Lost Valley
McCracken and the Lost City
McCracken and the Lost Lagoon

MCCRACKEN
AND THE
LOST LADY

By Mark Adderley

Yankton, South Dakota
2017

Published by Scriptorium Press,
Yankton, South Dakota

To Mary
Who Did Most of the Writing Anyway

Contents

I knew it was going to be a bad day when I saw the squadron of Albatross D.IIIs turn in their check-mark formation and fly directly towards us.

The D.III is a beautiful aircraft, sleek and curved, highly manoeuvrable and fast. The Austro-Hungarian air force, the *Luftfahrtruppen*, compromised the streamlined beauty of the aeroplanes by removing the spinner, which had a tendency otherwise to fall off in flight. That produced a stubbier nose than the variants flown by German pilots on the Western Front. But that didn't alter the speed of the planes or the deadliness of their armaments. I looked over my shoulder, catching the attention of Vasili Ivanovich Sikorsky, my Ukrainian friend who was actually piloting our aircraft. I pointed towards the approaching enemies. Sikorsky nodded to indicate that he had seen them.

We were flying a Macchi M.4, built by the Italian aircraft manufacturer Aeronautica Macchi. The M.4 is a fine plane, but it's multi-purpose, designed to carry bombs, reconnoitre enemy positions or land on water using the large floats suspended beneath its lower wings. At a pinch, it could also act as a fighter. In addition to this, Sikorsky and I had adapted this machine, placing a passenger, who could observe ground-troops and man the forward-pointing machine-gun, in front of the pilot. We were therefore heavier, and this made us a lot slower than the D.IIIs. We would have to have our wits about us.

The D.IIIs were gaining on us. I glanced back at Sikorsky again. At this point, it was unlikely we'd be able to outrun the Austrian planes, and Sikorsky was probably planning something. I wished I could ask him what was on his mind, but the roar of the engine, suspended from the upper wings, made all conversation impossible.

The nose of the M.4 began to turn. The right wing dipped. We were turning *towards* the enemy fighters.

Crazy Ukrainian! I thought, quickly touching the Rosary I carried in my breast pocket and offering a prayer to Our Lady. I thumbed the machine-gun's safety off and, as the D.IIIs swung into vision, lined up my sights on the plane in front.

The guns of the lead Albatross flickered and bullets whizzed past my ears, but I didn't open fire yet. This was probably the most unnerving part of aerial combat. Wait until you're close enough to be sure of making a hit.

The leader's two wing-men opened up, firing a couple of brief bursts. A long burst would often jam the machine-guns, especially since they tended to freeze anyway. I heard several bullets tear through the wood and canvas frame of our M.4.

The wings of the oncoming D.IIIs almost disappeared against the bright sky behind them, but I could see everything else. I could see the yawning muzzles of the guns, I could see the goggles and flying helmets of the pilots. They were close enough.

I squeezed the trigger, risking a long burst and, sure enough, my gun jammed. But I saw smoke belch out of the engine of the lead aeroplane, thick and black and cloying.

As soon as Sikorsky saw my hit, he pushed the control column forward and the nose of the M.4 dropped sharply. The Albatrosses slipped upwards out of my sight, and I saw the green fields and azure lakes of the borderlands between Austria and Switzerland. We had been on a reconnaissance mission over Austrian positions, and had just headed back towards our home base in northern Italy when the enemy squadron had pounced on us.

The ground swelled and grew enormous before us. The air streamed past my face. I could feel gravitational forces flattening me as we screamed downwards, faster and faster. The wings began to shake.

When I thought the plane couldn't take any more, Sikorsky eased up on the control column, and the M.4 swung upwards, carried partly by the 160-

horsepower engine, but mostly by the momentum he had built up.

For a moment, we climbed almost vertically, it seemed, until Sikorsky pumped the pedals that controlled the ailerons and we swung round in a wide half-circle.

We were right behind the Albatrosses, slightly below them and climbing. Seeing their vulnerability, they had begun to scatter. But Sikorsky dived straight for the nearest aeroplane. It dodged right, then left. I couldn't fix it in my sights. But its evasive manoeuvres also slowed it down, and we closed the distance between us rapidly. Back and forth it swooped, in and out of my cross-hairs.

"Stay still, will you!" I snarled under my breath.

I balled my fist and slammed it into the machine-gun to free the jam, then squeezed the trigger. Nothing happened. I slammed my gloved fist into it again, a couple of times. We were close now. I could see the exhaust pipe beside the cockpit, belching little puffs of black smoke. I could see the pilot's head turning to see where we were. I could see the rudder, emblazoned with the Maltese cross, moving back and forth. I squeezed the trigger again, and the gun fired, but I missed.

The D.III swung away and then back through my cross-hairs. My finger tensed.

The muzzle of my gun flashed and the harsh staccato coughing crashed through the drone of the engine. Bullets tore through the tail of the Albatross and shredded the left elevator and the rudder. The plane seemed to flip over slowly and it spun towards the ground. I prayed for the downed pilot. "We score victories, not kills," James McCuddon, a British ace, had told me. "We shoot down planes, not men."

I did a quick visual scan of the skies, and could see no trace of the other Austrian planes. But I did see something else: black streaks down the side of the housing of the Isotta Fraschini engine. A bullet from one of the Austrian planes had punctured the fuel line, and it was leaking petrol. I jabbed my forefinger at the damaged engine. Sikorsky looked up, then back at me, and nodded. He turned the M.4's nose, and glancing down at my compass, I saw he was heading southwest. He was taking us back to the aerodrome in Varese, in the north of Italy, our temporary home. I looked back up at Sikorsky; it was difficult to tell through the face-mask and the goggles, but he looked very determined. Varese was about a hundred miles away—easy enough with half a tank of fuel, but very dubious with a punctured fuel line.

I looked around my cockpit. There wasn't a lot in it, since it was not really my plane. But there was a rag, which I used for cleaning ice off the gun and the gauges. Stuffing it into my pocket, I rose in my seat and, grabbing the wire support that connected the fuselage with the leading edge of the upper wing, I climbed out of the cockpit and stepped backwards towards the wing.

Sikorsky glanced at me, but kept his focus rigidly forwards. He knew what I was up to, and was used to my ways.

The wind felt twenty times more powerful out of the cockpit than in it. The whole world seemed to vibrate, as if it were trying to knock me off the fragile machine and into the void. Below me, I could see fields and trees and tiny little roofs. Everyday life continued in Switzerland, while I contended with the elements up here.

I finally reached the wing, grabbing the strut that supported the engine with my hand, bracing my foot against it. The propeller spun about two feet away— it was one of those that faced backwards—and the wind and the engine's clamour were almost unbearable. But I could see where the fuel was leaking and, reaching up, I swiftly wrapped the line with the rag two or three times and tied a tight knot. It wouldn't stop the leak entirely, but it would slow it down, and possibly buy us a little extra time.

Gingerly, I started to reverse my course, and in a few moments was back inside my cockpit.

At that very moment, Sikorsky hit a pocket of warm air, and the plane jolted upwards. A moment earlier, I realized, that jolt would have tossed me from the plane and down to the ground, a thousand feet below. I touched the Rosary I kept in my breast pocket and said *thank you* quickly.

Over the next half hour, I kept my ear attuned to the sound of the engine. I began to think that perhaps we would be able to get home after all. But then the engine coughed, and I knew it was over. I glanced back at Sikorsky, and could tell that he knew it too. The engine sputtered a few times, then died. The propeller slowed to a stop. The world seemed suddenly eerie and quiet, and I heard Sikorsky behind me shout out: "Hold on, McCracken—we land in lake!"

Below us, I could see the lush green of the high mountain pastures that reminded me of the Land of Zun that we had visited a few years previously. The vivid blue of a lake, shot with gold from the sun, swung into view ahead of us. Could we glide that far? I wondered. If so, we could land on it too, but trying to land on the ground would destroy both the aircraft and us.

The M.4 began to pick up speed, the wind whistling past my ears. Sikorsky raised the flaps a little, to create drag and slow the plane, but the left elevator was jammed, and I could see, gazing towards the rear of the aircraft, that it had been damaged by enemy gunfire. We had taken worse hits than I had expected—only Sikorsky's flying and God's help had saved us from total disaster.

The lake was close now, and treetops flashed past fifty feet below. I held my breath. Our nose was pointing just a little short of the lake. I braced my feet against the front of my cockpit.

"Sikorsky," I called over my shoulder, "what are you doing?"

"Aiming for road," replied Sikorsky, yelling above the sound of the rushing wind. There was indeed a road running along the edge of the lake, like a long winding white ribbon.

"We can't land on the road!" I yelled back.

"Is correct," said Sikorsky. "But road is warmer than trees or water."

At that moment, the M.4 passed over the road and, as it did so, a warm updraft caught us under the wing surfaces and raised us ever so slightly. Grass rushed by underneath, and then water. I breathed again: Sikorsky had caught the updraft and gained us the few feet we needed to make it to the lake.

But now he cried out in alarm, and I saw that ahead of us was a small boat. A man, dressed in black, sat in the boat with a fishing rod, and our course took us on a collision course with him.

The ailerons moved and the plane banked left. With a *whoosh!* we sailed past the fishing boat, our wing-tip sluicing water up in a great fan. The fishing boat bobbed up and down in the waves but did not sink. Sikorsky struggled to correct the roll of the plane, but hitting the water with the wing-tip was irreversible. The plane bounced. The right wing crashed into the water and the nose ploughed forward. Its tail rose in a slow arc, then dropped into the lake. My world was suddenly freezing water. I kicked with my feet, struggling free of the cockpit. Disoriented for a moment, I looked for air bubbles—they would tell me which way was up. I followed the silvery spheres, kicking away from the sinking wreck of the plane and towards the surface. My flight jacket was thick and heavy, and it drank the icy waters of the lake so that swimming was laboursome. The weight of my boots began to drag me down. I tried to unfasten my jacket, but my fingers were thick inside my gloves. I pulled hard at them, but I could feel myself sinking through the frigid waters.

But then I felt hands grab me and haul me out of the water. A moment later, Sikorsky and I were sprawling in the bottom of the fishing boat we had just seen. The man in black, it turned out, was a Catholic priest, and he had set his fishing rod down in the bottom of the boat to pull us out of the water.

The priest offered us a little flask. It contained Cognac, and although I shivered with cold, it created a little warm place right in the middle of my body. I passed the flask on to Sikorsky.

"*Italieri?*" asked the priest.

I shook my head. "*Scozzese,*" I replied.

The priest laughed. "Scotsman," he said, "you have made me a fisher of men!"

CHAPTER 2
A MEETING IN SWITZERLAND

It turned out that Fr. Sebastien, the fisherman, was a priest in the diocese of Zurich, taking a few days' leave in a tiny cottage on the shore of the lake into which we had deposited our aeroplane. He took us, dripping and shivering, to the cottage and lit a fire, which was soon roaring in the grate, then gave us each a blanket so that we could hang up our soaking clothes to dry. Once he had made sure we were recovering, he put on a pot of coffee and filleted the fish he had caught. Before long, the delightful aroma of frying fish filled the single room of the cottage.

"You must pardon me for asking," Fr. Sebastien said, when we had told him our story, "but what brings a Scotsman and a Russian to Switzerland, in an Italian aeroplane, pursued by members of the Austrian Air Force?"

"Not Russian—Ukrainian," corrected Sikorsky.

"*Pardonnez-moi*," answered Fr. Sebastien, pouring coffee into three mugs and handing us each one, "*Ukranien.*"

"I'm an engineer," I explained. "I work for the British aeroplane manufacturer, Vickers-Armstrong. They're in partnership with an Italian company,

Aeronautica Macchi, and I came to Italy to help develop navigational systems for reconnaisance planes. I asked for Sikorsky's help because he's a good friend and the best aviator I know."

"*Spasiba*," said Sikorsky, with a nod.

Fr. Sebastien looked at Sikorsky for a long time. It seemed he was reflecting deeply on something. At length, he asked, "As a Ukrainian, Vasili Ivanovich, are you indifferent to news from Russia? I know there has been much tension between Russia and the Ukraine for many years."

"*Da*." Sikorsky nodded his agreement. "My countrymen cannot even decide on which side to fight in this War. Is worse than civil war! But I know the Romanovs—two times I have flown my aeroplane for them. What is news from Russia?"

Fr. Sebastien walked over to a table, picking up a folded newspaper. "You have heard of the attempted revolution?"

Sikorsky gave a long sigh. "The people, they protest that Russia fights this War. They have suffered much. This revolution, it has been very violent. Many people have been killed. But it was not successful, I think."

"Not successful," agreed Fr. Sebastien. After a moment's thought, he handed the newspaper to Sikorsky. "But still there are many consequences." Sikorsky unfolded the newspaper. It was called *La Nouvelliste*, and the front page carried a headline I couldn't understand, as it was in French, accompanied by a line drawing of Tsar Nicholas. Sikorsky, however, like many Ukrainians and Russians, was fluent in French, and gave a gasp of shock.

"Nikolai!" he cried. "The Tsar—he *otrekayetsya*." He gave a small grunt of frustration. "What is word? He give up being tsar."

"He's abdicated?" I was as amazed as my Ukrainian friend.

"*Da*—he abdicate."

"So . . . who is the tsar now?" I asked.

"There is no tsar." Sikorsky ran a hand over his forehead. "This is end of age—for three hundred years the Romanovs have ruled Russia." Frowning, he added, "I do not think is it quite *pravovoy*—legal."

"Legal or illegal, it has happened," Fr. Sebastien pointed out. "You cannot make a king rule who does not wish to rule. A provisional government has been appointed for Russia, and the people will decide whether they want the monarchy to continue or change to a republic."

"A choice is good, isn't it?" I asked anxiously.

Sikorsky puffed out his cheeks. "Russian people—they do not do well with choices."

Fr. Sebastien placed a reassuring hand on Sikorsky's shoulder. "Forgive me for bringing you these ill news, Vasili Ivanovich. The world has become a topsy-turvy place, I think. Men have made it so. But there is still a God in Heaven, who seeks to guide us through the ruins of our civilization towards Him. It is to Him we must look now, gentlemen." He took out a small black case that looked like an oversized briefcase. "Now, however, you gentlemen must excuse me. I am on holiday, but I am still a priest, and must celebrate Mass. If either of you is Catholic, you are welcome to join me."

So we joined Fr. Sebastien for Mass, and spent the night in his cottage, warm and comfortable before the sinking embers of the fire. In the morning, he set us on our road with advice on how we could reach Berne, where the British ambassador could find a way of getting us back to Italy, and I could cable my wife, Ariadne, to let her know we were safe. Fr. Sebastien provided us with food, but could not give us a ride, as he had only his own bicycle with him.

We hitched a ride with a hay cart for part of the way, then walked for a couple of hours. In the high meadows, there weren't many villages, though we were surrounded by cultivated fields, in most of which grazed contented-looking brown and white cows, their bells tolling gently as they moved their heads to and fro.

When the sun began to sink, we had still not reached a town from which we could catch a train to Berne. The shadows began to grow all around us, and the first stars pierced the lavender canopy of evening. It was then we saw a little yellow light wobbling towards us, like a will o' th' wisp. It turned out to be a man on a bicycle. Sikorsky, waving his arms high, stepped out into the road in front of the man, who stopped beside us. For a few moments, Sikorsky and the cyclist spoke to one another in French. In the end, Sikorsky turned to me.

"This man, he says he has small cottage nearby. For fifty francs, we can sleep in it for the night. He will come back tomorrow with horse and cart, and take us to town where we can catch train to Berne."

"Fifty francs!" I exploded. "I could buy a house for that much! Anyway, we don't have any Swiss money."

"Not quite buy house." Sikorsky wagged a cautionary finger at me. "Do not exaggerate, McCracken. Man's fee is very great, but is only option. And he take us where we need to go tomorrow. I will see if he will take Italian money."

The man was grinning—I could just make out his face in the light from the bicycle. "I don't like it," I grumbled, "but I suppose we don't have a choice about it."

The cyclist led us a little further along the road, then pointed down a dirt track.

"He says cottage is down here." Sikorsky shrugged and paid the man in lire. The man went off on his bicycle, and I could have sworn I heard him laughing as he went.

The night was dark, as there were no street lights, but that meant the stars were brilliant overhead, and by their light we could just perceive the outline of a ramshackle barn. The walls were not straight, and I could see a hole in the roof as we neared it.

"Just a barn in the middle of nowhere and no cottage," I mused, looking around for any sign of a residence, and finding none. "I think that cyclist took advantage of us." I gave a sigh. "Well, why not take the adventure God sends?"

The barn was in even worse repair than we had expected. It smelled of damp and cow manure, and the wind rattled through cracks in the wall planking. I had not noticed that it was windy when we were outside, but what little wind there was made a big difference inside the barn.

We sat down and unwrapped the last of the bread and cheese Fr. Sebastien had given us. Sikorsky gave me his cheese, as he doesn't really like it unless it's an ingredient in something else, and we ate in silence. Finally, we settled down to sleep in the hayloft. It was scratchy but warm, and I slept as soundly as a man who's spent all day outside usually sleeps.

I was awoken by the horizontal rays of the sun thrusting like axles through the hayloft's window. For a few moments I lay there, wondering where I was. Then slowly the events of the previous day crowded into my mind.

Outside the barn, I heard the sound of a combustion engine dying. Somebody had just switched off the engine of a motor-car—a smooth-sounding engine with four cylinders. I crawled over to the window, where I joined Sikorsky, who was already awake and staring with narrowed eyes through the window, just as a motor-car door slammed.

Below us, two uniformed men had just climbed down from the back of a 1910 Gräf and Stift Double Phaeton limousine. The chauffeur, a corporal in the Austro-Hungarian infantry, was just climbing back into his seat behind the wheel as his two passengers strolled towards the barn. They wore officers' greatcoats and peaked caps, but one was grey, the other light olive green. I puzzled over this for a moment, because I had never seen a Russian officer before, whereas I had seen quite a few Austrians. But it was odd to see the two together, as the Russians were still on the Allied side in the War, and therefore enemies with the Austro-Hungarian Empire. Still, these two seemed to be friends. They spoke together in French, laughing occasionally, and having reached the shelter of the barn, the Austrian pulled out a packet of cigarettes and lit one for each of them.

Sikorsky leaned close to me. "They wait for someone," he explained in a whisper. "I cannot tell who."

It was then we heard another noise: a second motor-car approached along the dirt road. It was nothing as fancy as the limousine; in fact, it looked a little disheveled, with dents in the body-work, patches on the tyres, and one of the mud-guards rattling as if loose. The car stopped beside the limousine, the engine died, and two men climbed out of the front seats. One of them was huge, almost seven feet tall, with a face that was all knobbles, like a ginger root. He reached into his pocket and took out of pair of iron spheres. They looked like low calibre cannon-balls. He began to run them around in his fingers as if they were no more than marbles.

The other newcomer was a man in his forties with a neat, triangular beard and a bald head. He looked a lot like a cartoon Satan. Sikorsky gasped.

"McCracken!" His voice rasped. "Do you know who that is?"

I shook my head. Below us, the Russian officer strode forward and embraced the newcomer, kissing him on either cheek as was the Russian custom. The Austrian officer held out his hand, which the new-comer seized and shook with such vigour that the Austrian winced and flexed his fingers afterwards.

"That is very bad man indeed, very bad man," muttered Sikorsky. "His name is Vladimir Ilyich Ulyanov."

I shrugged. I had never heard of him. "Who is this Ulyanov?" I whispered.

"He is leader of new political movement." Sikorsky leaned in close, still keeping his eye on the group below. "They believe in crazy things—government should own all things and give workers wages."

"He's a communist?"

"*Da.* Bolshevik. That in Russian means *greater, stronger.* If you are stronger, you can do many things, many bad things to people."

"I've still never heard of him."

"He has other name, name from river where he was in prison. Ulyanov is old name. Now, this man, he calls himself Lenin."

CHAPTER 3

A REVOLUTIONARY PLOT

I had heard of Vladimir Ilyich Lenin, the famous
communist revolutionary. He had been arrested
and imprisoned, exiled, and kicked out of many
other countries, spending a lot of time in England
trying to organize a revolution in his Russian home-
land. I didn't know much else about him but it was
certainly interesting to see him in this company, and
I wondered what on earth was going on. Sikorsky
and I both craned forward, our ears pricked, though
I don't know why—I had no idea what they were
saying. They spoke in French most of the time, but
Lenin and his countryman occasionally resorted to
Russian, and Lenin and the Austrian officer sometimes spoke in German. Sometimes they laughed.
The huge, ugly man played with the cannonballs,
sometimes rolling them round the palm of one huge
hand, sometimes rolling them up to his elbow,
sometimes passing them from one hand to the other
as if they had wills of their own. Sometimes Lenin
would get carried away. His voice would rise with
anger, and he would stab his forefinger at the others,
or at imaginary enemies. Once, he pulled the cigarette out of the Austrian officer's mouth and ground
it under his foot with a long and angry speech deliv-

ered inches from the officer's face. At one point, they all strode to the limousine and the Austrian officer smoothed out a map on the bonnet.

"This is amazing!" Sikorsky whispered, leaning close to me. "This Austrian officer, he wants to take Lenin all the way to Russia, to start revolution."

"Another one!" I was a little surprised. "How many revolutions does one country need?"

Suddenly, the big man stopped juggling and pocketed the cannonballs. He leaned over to Lenin and whispered something in his ear. Lenin nodded. Quietly, while the others continued to talk, the big man tiptoed over to a bush. He waited a moment then, like a frog's tongue, his arm shot into the bush and pulled.

Dangling from his immense fist was the cyclist who had conned us out of fifty francs last night. He squirmed and pleaded and whined. The huge man dropped the cyclist in front of Lenin and the others.

"They want to know why he listens to them," Sikorsky said *sotto voce*.

"He must have come to get us," I replied. "I wonder why he hasn't brought the horse and cart?"

The men down below had surrounded the cyclist, who was on his knees, jabbering away, his face turning from one to another of them. The huge man had the cannonballs out again. They hopped from one hand to the other, across the backs of his hands, up to his elbows. The cyclist prattled on. In the end, he thrust his arm out towards the barn.

"*Bozhe moi!*" hissed Sikorsky. "This man, he will betray us!"

The four men below parted, leaving a gap so that the cyclist could escape. Lenin's arm was out, as if indicating that the cyclist should leave as quickly as possible. The Austrian officer folded up the map and slipped it into the inside pocket of his greatcoat. The cyclist scrambled to his feet and sped away down the dirt track.

Lenin's eyes turned towards the big man. The man stopped manipulating the cannonballs. He held one in each hand. One arm rose. His wrist flicked. The ball flew from it. With a sharp crack and a cry of pain, the cyclist spun into the long grass at the side of the dirt track.

Sikorsky gasped. Making the Sign of the Cross, he began praying the *Ave Maria*. I had covered my mouth. My eyes were wide but I could not take them off the scene below

The huge man walked up the dirt road to where the cyclist lay. He made a quick examination of the body, pocketed the cannonball, and called something to Lenin.

"Rabotnik!" cried Lenin, "*idi syuda!*"

The big man started walking slowly back towards the group, while Lenin got more and more frustrated. He spouted a stream of angry Russian that excited Rabotnik to a shuffle barely quicker than his walking had been. Lenin's finger stabbed towards the barn again and again.

Sikorsky drew away from the window. "He tells Rabotnik, the big man, to search barn."

There wasn't anything else we could do. We prayed the Hail Mary, over and over again, under our breath.

The barn door creaked open on its rusty hinges and Rabotnik entered. He gripped one of the cannonballs in each massive palm. His head moved sluggishly left and right. At any moment, his eye would light upon the ladder that led up to the hayloft. The cannonball spun idly in his hand as he peered into one corner after another.

At a noise, Rabotnik stepped over to a shuttered window, pushed it open and peered outside. But it was just the wind blowing the shutter. There was nothing to see but the meadow and the mountains, so he redirected his attention to the barn's interior. It was then he spied the ladder.

At that moment, the sun peered through the window behind us. It shone right into Rabotnik's eyes and he squinted. Sikorsky gasped and pointed.

The sun had cast a shadow across the floor of the barn next to Rabotnik, and it looked exactly like the outline of a tall and gracious lady. Rabotnik twitched, as if he felt a sudden twinge of pain. He took a step backwards, out of the sunlight, and peered round as if trying to remember something. Then he turned towards the door and, a moment later, was gone.

I looked back at the shadow. It was perfectly normal, just a shadow cast by a large blower such as had once been used at a blacksmith's forge. For a moment, it had certainly looked like the shadow of a lady.

With a sigh of relief, Sikorsky and I turned our attention to the scene outside. The group was saying goodbye to one another, while Rabotnik dropped the still form of the cyclist into the boot of the car in which he and Lenin had arrived. Cigarettes were extinguished, hands were shaken, cheeks kissed, and the four men climbed into their motor-cars. One or two turns on the cranks, and a pair of engines roared as the cars rattled down the dirt road. Sikorsky and I climbed down from the hayloft and watched the motor-cars dwindle in different directions.

"Why would they want him to start another revolution in Russia?" I wondered.

Sikorsky gave a sad shake of his head. "If this man Lenin can start revolution, Russia will get out of War. Then, Germany and Austria can send troops from East, where they fight Russia, to Western Front, where they fight Britain and France."

"That would totally overwhelm the Allies!" I cried in alarm.

"That is their plan. They take Lenin by train in sealed car to St. Petersburg. There, he will lead people in Bolshevik revolution."

"Can he succeed?"

Sikorsky considered the question for a moment. The cars were now totally gone from sight. "Russia has seen many revolutions. February Revolution just failed. Another revolution back in '05. Russian people, they are tired, they want change, they want freedom and no more war."

"We all want this War to end," I pointed out.

"This Lenin, he will promise the people he will end War. He is fanatic. He does not rest, does not sleep. All he thinks is revolution. If anyone can lead successful revolution, Lenin can."

"Then we have to tell someone about this at once," I said. Sikorsky nodded his vigorous agreement, and we quickly gathered our belongings. A few minutes later, we were on the road again.

Soon, we found a tiny village nestling in the lap of a green valley. From there, we were able to take a train to Berne, where I cabled my wife and we made our report to the British ambassador, who thanked us and put us on yet another train, which carried us on a winding route through much the same country we had just traveled, and eventually deposited us in Varese. We took a taxi to the aerodrome, where Sikorsky lived on board the LS3, the airship we had acquired several years earlier.

"You will come aboard LS3, McCracken?" wondered Sikorsky. "I have very fine vodka. And whisky too, and many cigars."

"Later, perhaps," I assured him. "I have to see Ari first, and Archie."

"Ah, Ariadne is very beautiful lady. If I were married, I would want to see wife too. *Do svidaniya*, McCracken! It has been very great adventure, as always."

"Well, knowing Vickers-Armstrong and Aeronautica Macchi," I replied, "it's likely to be as great an adventure tomorrow! See you later, Sikorsky."

As the taxi pulled away, bumping over the cobblestones, I created in my mind a cozy little picture of my family in the house Vickers-Armstrong had rented for me in town. Ari, my beautiful dark-haired American wife, would perhaps be reading by gas-light, while my fifteen-month-old son Archie would be constructing large edifices with his wooden blocks. Perhaps Fritz, our German servant, would hover in the doorway to announce that supper was served in the *Speiseraum*, the word he invariably used for *dining room*. Perhaps some music would be playing softly from the gramophone.

The taxi rolled to a halt and I climbed out, dropping a few coins into the driver's palm. "*Grazie*," he said and pulled away.

The house we lived in while we were in Varese was a three-story building, painted in peeling tangerine. The pavement outside the front door was covered by a portico. I realized that I had lost my key somewhere on my travels, and looking up at the darkening sky, wondered if I would disturb anyone by knocking on the door.

With a rush of emotion, I suddenly realized how wonderful it would be to see Fritz open the door. He was short, wall-eyed and red-haired, of very remarkable appearance, but it would be overwhelmingly good to see him again, for everything to be normal again. I raised my hand and rapped three times on the door with my knuckles.

After a short pause, the door opened.

It was not Fritz who stood there, but a tall gentleman in a black suit and tails, a grey waistcoat and a starched collar. His head was mostly bald, pink and shiny, and a thin moustache faintly outlined his upper lip.

My lower jaw dropped.

"Master McCracken," said the gentleman, "how very pleasant to see you. I shall announce your arrival to her ladyship at once."

"Hogarth!" screeched a voice from inside the house. "*Hogarth!*"

"Great Scott!" I gasped, reeling under a sudden realization. "Aunt Polly's here!"

CHAPTER 4
A RELATIVE INCONVENIENCE

Hogarth," I said, when I had sufficiently recovered from my shock, "what are you doing here?"

The butler stepped aside to allow me to enter. "Serving her ladyship as usual, sir. May I take your coat?"

I shrugged my shoulders out of my flight jacket and handed it to him. As he was hanging it on a hook, my wife Ariadne appeared in the hallway. Her natural beauty was mixed with anxiety as she ran forward and flung her arms about me.

"I see you've met Hogarth," she said in a whisper.

"Years ago," I answered. "I'm astounded to see him here now."

"Your Aunt Polly is here." Ari steered me towards the parlour, behind the slow-moving and stately Hogarth. "She's driving me crazy, not to mention poor Fritz."

"Fritz?"

"She's a very exacting eater—as you probably remember."

"She has her own chef," I pointed out, "a little Italian called Raimondo. Or perhaps that's the problem? Why is she here?"

The anxiety was briefly replaced by guilt on Ari's face. "You remember that she was at our wedding?"

I closed my eyes and drew a hand across them. "You invited her, didn't you?" Ari nodded. "How's Archie?"

"Asleep," she replied. "Though with all this noise—"

"Hogarth!" came a strident voice from the parlour. "Hogarth, where are you? Who was at the door? Confound the man! Hogarth!"

"Forgive me, ma'am," Hogarth said, entering the room ahead of us, "young Master McCracken has arrived."

"Well, it's about time!"

My Aunt Polly is a tall, slender lady of about sixty years, who looks as if her smile has been glued on upside-down. She always wears a green dress, which is curious, since her last name is Green, and carries a cherry-wood cane with a golden top. Her late husband, Major General Griffin Fortescue-Green, had died with a restful smile on his face twenty years ago, and since then she had been dividing her time between winter months in Amalfi on the Adriatic coast of Italy and summers in her houses in Chelsea and Littleford-on-the-Ouse. On seeing me, her face lit up. I was the only one of her many nephews whom she could tolerate.

"Crackers!" she enthused, holding out her arms to receive my embrace and a peck on the cheek, "how perfectly divine to see you!"

"Aunt Polly, you know I don't like that nick-name."

She pinched my cheek between her forefinger and thumb and squeezed it with what I presume she reckoned to be affection. "Have I told you the story of his third birthday?" she asked of the world in general. "There we were—his mother and father, General Green and I, and in comes young Crackers, covered with mud, and says with all seriousness, 'I am three and I am McCracken!' Just like that, the precious little darling!" She sighed. "That was thirty-six years ago now, and my husband was still alive, God rest his soul." She made the Sign of the Cross.

"What are you doing here, Aunt Polly?"

"Returning to England. And you're the only person in Italy who can help me. They won't let me on a boat. I tried at the port, and I tried the embassy in Rome."

"Aunt Polly, there is a war on."

"That's what that impertinent young man at the embassy said. Do something, Crackers, do something!"

"You understand, don't you, Aunt Polly, that there are U-boats all over the place."

"What has that got to do with me?" asked Aunt Polly in all innocence.

"Well, U-boats, you see . . . they torpedo ships. They sink them."

"They wouldn't dare!" roared Aunt Polly, puffing out her chest and seeming to grow six inches.

"If they knew you they wouldn't, that's certain."

"Are you being impertinent, Crackers?" Aunt Polly glared at me over her pince-nez. "Well, it doesn't matter. Find me passage back to England. And don't tell me you can't do it—I know you can. Take Grubworthy with you."

"Grubworthy?"

"My private secretary, Crackers, my private secretary! Really!"

An immensely fat man, who had been sitting on our sofa and consuming with almost mechanical precision a series of cucumber sandwiches, got to his feet. A blizzard of breadcrumbs tumbled from his chest as he did so. He wiped the palm of his hand on the seat of his trousers.

"Cadwallader Grubworthy," he said. His hand was still faintly sticky.

Before I could say anything in reply, Aunt Polly proclaimed: "Crackers, I need your chef. How much does he require?"

"Fritz? I don't know. I don't think he's for hire."

"Nonsense. I need a chef."

"She does." Grubworthy reached for another cucumber sandwich. There were very few left. "And he's very good."

"What happened to Raimondo?" I asked.

Aunt Polly threw up her hands. "Impossible man! That's the problem with Italians—temperamental, all of them. He just walked out, without a word of warning."

"She threw a bowl of soup at him." Grubworthy popped the last cucumber sandwich into his mouth. "Lobster bisque."

"That's no reason to leave the service of a woman of substance," returned Aunt Polly, "and I'll remind you to keep your opinions to yourself, Grubworthy." She underscored her words by prodding Grubworthy sharply on the shoulder with the tip of her cane.

"My aim is to please you in all things, m'lady." Grubworthy bobbed his head in a funny little bow and dropped back onto the sofa, which groaned under his weight.

"Hogarth!" screeched Aunt Polly, and we all jumped. "*Hogarth!*"

A second later, Hogarth stood in the doorway. "Ma'am?"

"Where is Inge?"

"In her room, ma'am."

"Is she crying again?"

"I really couldn't say, ma'am."

"Tell her to come here at once."

"As you wish, ma'am."

"Is Inge still with you, Aunt Polly?" Inga was the tall Swedish chambermaid who had been with Aunt Polly for almost a decade now. She was always moving from one personal crisis to another.

"She's in love with a red-haired Welshman," remarked Aunt Polly bitterly, as if all moral decrepitude were summed up in the situation. "A *short* red-haired Welshman. No good can come of it. I told her so, but she won't listen. That's Swedes for you."

My head was beginning to swim. I said, "Aunt Polly, will you please excuse me? I need to refresh myself—I've had a long journey."

"Very well." Aunt Polly held out her hand for me to kiss. "We dine at eight, and don't forget to dress."

"Is she always like this?" asked Ari, as we went up the stairs. On the second floor, two doors led off a tiny passageway. I creaked open one door and peered in the sleeping form of Archie, his outline softened by the bed-blankets. One pudgy hand trailed on the floor. Our newly-acquired cat Edison slept peacefully at the foot of the bed. Various building toys lay scattered over the floor. The curtains wafted gently in a breeze through the open window.

"She's always like this," I answered with a sigh, "except when she's asleep." I closed the door softly. "Aunt Polly hates all women and most men, but for some reason she dotes on me. I don't understand it, and it's really very inconvenient."

"Well, an inconvenience is just—"

"An adventure, wrongly considered. Yes, I know. Right now, though, I need a little peace, before I dress for dinner. What's that about, by the way? We never dine formally."

"When we're in someone else's home we do."

"Right. And when Aunt Polly visits, it's her house. What's this?"

Ari had been holding a calling card in her hand and she held it out to me now. "A gentleman called for you earlier today. I've read some of his poems."

"He's a poet?" I read the front of the card:

SIR RENNELL RODD, CB, KCMG, GCVO, GCMG
POET, SCHOLAR, DIPLOMAT
AND HIS BRITANNIC MAJESTY'S AMBASSADOR
TO THE KINGDOM OF ITALY

Flipping it over, I saw that the visitor had scrawled on the back: "I need to see you at once, on an urgent matter. I shall call again tomorrow morning. Please invite your wife and Mr. Sikorsky. R. R."

"Poet and scholar? What on earth could he want?"

Ari shrugged. "We'll find out tomorrow, I guess."

"Well, at least Sir Rennell Rodd will provide some relief from Aunt Polly," I said, and we both laughed.

At breakfast the following morning, Aunt Polly pressed her suit once more to Fritz, which caused an outpouring of German too fast for even Ari to follow, despite her vast and fluent knowledge of so many languages. When he had left the dining room, Aunt Polly asked, "I assume he makes chocolate?"

"Chocolate?"

"Don't all Swiss chefs make chocolate?"

"Fritz isn't Swiss, Aunt Polly. He's German."

A shocked silence ensued, during which I spread some rich butter and strawberry jam on my toasted brioche and enjoyed the silence.

"Is that really the thing, Crackers dear?" wondered Aunt Polly. "After all, there is a war on, you know."

"I know, Aunt Polly, but Fritz has been with us since before the War, and his family is still in Germany—his wife and fourteen children."

"Fourteen children!" Aunt Polly was clearly shocked. "That seems a little excessive, don't you think? One might have four children and consider it quite normal. But fourteen seems a trifle enthusiastic. It smacks of jazz music or some other unwarranted pastime."

I continued to eat my toasted brioche in silence, thinking about how much I really love its lightness, its sweetness, its delicacy. Sipping my espresso, I reminded myself to congratulate Fritz on an excellent Italian breakfast.

While Fritz and a sniffling Inge cleared away the breakfast things, I went upstairs to find my pocket watch. It was on the nightstand, but had stopped during the night, so I consulted the big clock in the hallway to set it right, and began winding it up. As I did so, someone knocked at the door. Fritz appeared, but Hogarth got there first.

"Sir Rennell Rodd to see you, Master McCracken."

"Show him in, Hogarth."

"Into the parlour, sir?"

I peered through the door into the parlour. Aunt Polly sat in the window, perfectly still. No one else was in the room. She held a photograph in her hand, and I thought it was of Major General Fortescue-Green. Softly, a little guiltily, I drew the door shut.

"Better show him in somewhere else, Hogarth," I suggested. "How about the kitchen?"

"Indeed, sir," returned Hogarth, with a slight emphasis. "This way, please, Sir Rennell."

"Have you eaten breakfast, Sir Rennell?" I asked as we shook hands and followed Hogarth down some steps.

"As a matter of fact I have, old man," replied Sir Rennell. He sniffed the air. The aroma of brioche still lingered, like a promise. "Still, let's keep an open mind, shall we?"

Grubworthy sat at the kitchen table, tossing a slice of brioche into his mouth like an engineer tossing coal into a firebox. Swallowing quickly, he said, "Hello there, McCracken. I was just helping Fritz with a few of the kitchen chores."

"*Ja*," interjected Fritz, "I could not that cup have washed without your assistance, Herr Grubworthy."

"I'm at your service to do more if necessary," offered Grubworthy, rising. He noticed a small dot of jam on his tie and rubbed at it, sucking his finger at intervals.

"Would you excuse us a moment, please, Grubworthy?" I asked, pulling out a chair for Sir Rennell.

"Not at all," answered Grubworthy distractedly, still focused on his tie. "Nothing for it, I'll have to change it. Fritz, can you clean my tie? I'll return the favour any time you wish."

"I think Inge can manage that," I said. Firmly, I added, "Good morning, Grubworthy."

"What? Oh yes. Good morning, McCracken."

No sooner had the door closed behind Grubworthy's expansive back than it opened again and Hogarth announced, "Mr. Vasili Sikorsky," and in came Sikorsky and Ari.

After the introductions had been made, we all sat about the little table and Sir Rennell said, "You seem to have a full house, McCracken."

"When my family visits, it's more like an invasion."

Sir Rennell cast his eyes around the narrow little kitchen. "Perhaps Vickers-Armstrong should find you a larger place?"

"Most of the time, it's too big for us," smiled Ari.

Fritz poured us each a cup of coffee and produced a loaf of brioche with jam and butter. "This from Herr Grubworthy I hid," he confided.

"I say." Sir Rennell leaned in close and dropped his voice to a whisper when Fritz had turned away to finish the washing-up. "Your man is German?"

I always seemed to be explaining this. "He's been with us since 1913. He's always our partner in adventure."

"He's completely loyal," added Ari.

"Jolly good." Sir Rennell nodded wisely. "You have to be careful, though—spies everywhere." He rose from his seat, opened the door a crack and peered out. Then he checked through the little window and, when he was satisfied there were no eavesdroppers around, resumed his seat. "I understand your man is no spy, of course, but one must take precautions." He sat back and bit into the brioche. "I say, this is most awfully good stuff. Did you bake this, Fritz?" Fritz nodded. "Well, my compliments, my compliments." Sir Rennell ate for a few moments in silence then, opening his attaché case and pulling out a sheaf of papers, he said, "Mr. and Mrs.

McCracken, Mr. Sikorsky, I am His Majesty's Ambassador to the Kingdom of Italy, and in my official role I read just a couple of days ago of the remarkable conversation you overheard recently in Switzerland." I nodded. "Do you know who the various interlocutors were?"

"I know one of them was Lenin."

"The name of the Austrian officer," added Sikorsky, "was Von Krems."

Sir Rennell nodded. "We've been able to identify him as Hauptman Franz-August Kunstler Von Krems."

"*Hauptman*?" I asked.

"It is the word that means *captain*, Herr McCracken," Fritz explained helpfully.

"Starting a revolution in Russia—it's an ambitious plot for a captain, isn't it?" I wondered.

"Von Krems is a young man, and very ambitious," explained Sir Rennell. "He's also connected by marriage to Kaiser Wilhelm's family. That's probably why he felt comfortable arranging that meeting with his friend Lenin."

"His friend?"

Sir Rennell nodded. "They met in London, in late 1903. You see, Von Krems' parents had been estranged almost from his birth, but they couldn't obtain a divorce in Austria. So they traveled to London. Lenin was there for the—" He opened a file and ran a finger down a page until he found the information he wanted. "Lenin was in London for the Second Congress of the Russian Social Democratic Labour Party."

Ari was skeptical. "A communist revolution," she said doubtfully. "It doesn't sound like the kind of thing the Kaiser would approve of."

"Probably not," replied Sir Rennell. "But the Kaiser would certainly approve of being able to re-deploy his troops from the Eastern to the Western Front. It would give Germany the advantage there." He leaned across the table and spoke very earnestly. "Mr. McCracken, our spies in Vienna have discov-ered the route that Mr. Lenin will be taking. He is to leave Zurich in a sealed train and travel north to Sassnitz, where he will take a ferry to Trelleborg in Sweden. From there, it seems, he will take another ferry to St. Petersburg, where he is to start the revo-lution."

"What would you like us to do?" I asked.

"Isn't it obvious? We want you to stop that train from reaching Sassnitz."

"You want us to kidnap Lenin?" Ari asked. Si-korsky burst out into laughter. "How?"

Sir Rennell shrugged. "You have a zeppelin, Mr. McCracken—the one you obtained from Baron Ho-henstaufen back in 1913. It would take but a small amount of black paint to make it look exactly like a German zeppelin. Catch that train, and bring back Lenin, before he can work his evil on poor Russia."

I thought about it for a moment. It looked like adventure had once more found me. Then an idea dawned upon me. "If I do this for you," I said slowly, "will you do me a favour in return?"

"Of course I shall, McCracken," answered Sir Rennell. "Name it."

I smiled. "Get my Aunt Polly passage back to England."

CHAPTER 5

THE STOWAWAY

The LS3, the airship we had acquired on a previous adventure, lay at rest under the giant canopy specially erected for her at Varese's aerodrome. She came in two parts. The envelope, which looked like a gigantic silver pencil about four hundred feet long, contained the huge ballonets, each one filled with hydrogen to provide the lift she needed to fly. The gondola, slung beneath the envelope and towards the front, contained our living quarters and work spaces. In some ways, the gondola was a bit like an ocean liner, with cabins, a wheelhouse, a dining room, a library, a workshop and a carriage house where we stored our 1910 Daimler. In an emergency, the gondola could be detached and used as a boat.

The beginning of an adventure is always an exciting time, but also very busy. We had supplies to load aboard the LS3, spare fuel, food, and our belongings from the house in Varese. A scaffold had been erected under the envelope and a crew was painting black Maltese Crosses on it amidships.

Entering the cabin Ari and I always took, I found a wristwatch on the night-stand and cried out in surprise. "I thought I'd lost this in Prester John's

Land!" I exclaimed. "It's my water-resistant wrist-watch!"

"I found it in one of the drawers," explained Ari. "No, darling—no jumping on the bed. Remember what happened to the monkeys?"

Thinking hard about the song we had sung with him so many times, Archie replied: "Monkeys jumping onna bed."

"And what happened to the monkeys, dear?"

"Fella bed, bumpa head."

"So what will happen to Archie?"

"Artie jumpa bed bumpa head." Suddenly, a horrified look came over Archie's face and he wailed: "Artie's a monkey!"

We were laughing hard when the door opened and Fritz entered, a sour look on his face and Edison in his hands. He dropped it onto the floor of our cabin. "Your cat, *Herr und Frau*," he said and, turning, he marched away.

Ari picked up the cat and started stroking him along his back. "Fritz doesn't care for Edison," she mused. "He keeps jumping on the tables in the galley and stealing food."

"I told you we should have got a dog," I remarked bitterly; that was an argument I had lost. Come to think of it, I couldn't remember an argument I'd won.

"You can't take a dog on an airship," replied Ari. "You'd have to land every couple of hours to let it do its business." Archie grabbed a bunch of Edison's whiskers in his pudgy hand and pulled. The cat extricated itself and jumped down from Ari's lap. "A cat is a perfect pet for adventurers."

A knock came from the door and once more Fritz put his head into the room. "Herr Rennell Rodd is in the *Speiseraum* and wishes to see you, Herr McCracken."

When Ari and I reached the dining room with Archie, we found that Sikorsky was already there and Fritz had served him and Sir Rennell drinks. The *Speiseraum* of the LS3 is at the very stern of the gondola, and the curved wall at the back is composed entirely of windows, so that as you fly you get a panoramic view of where you have come from. The room contained six teak tables with leatherbacked chairs. Fritz stood behind the bar, pouring me a whisky and Ari a glass of champagne.

"Good morning, Mr. McCracken!" beamed Sir Rennell as we joined him at the table. "I say, what a wonderful way of getting from place to place! Are you sure Mrs. Green wouldn't prefer to travel by airship rather than by sea?"

"She can't come with us, if that's what you mean," I answered.

"I suppose not. Just for your information, I've got her passage on the *RMS Gaelic*, which leaves for London in about a week."

"Thank you very much, Sir Rennell."

"Oh, you're most welcome, McCracken, most welcome indeed." He took a stack of papers out of a briefcase and set them down on the table, then raised his whisky. "Here's to a successful mission and a victorious conclusion to this wretched War." When we had all drunk the toast, he asked, "Do you have everything you need?"

Sikorsky held up a hand. "Flight plan is strange; we fly very far—through Germany and across North Sea to London."

"You have enough fuel, do you not?" asked Sir Rennell.

Sikorsky nodded. "But adventures are unpredictable. One slight deviation in course, and we have no fuel to return to London."

Sir Rennell gave a nod and a sigh. "I understand your concerns, Mr. Sikorsky," he said, "but fuel is in very short supply at this point in the War." Shuffling through the pile of papers, he found one. "This is a requisition order. You can refuel at any friendly aerodrome. But there's no more fuel to be had here, I'm afraid." Sir Rennell buckled the briefcase closed and set it on the floor beside his chair. "McCracken, I must be completely honest with you. This is a very dangerous business. The crosses we're painting on your zeppelin are a kind of disguise, and that means if you're captured whilst flying over enemy territory, you might well be treated as a spy, and shot."

"What would Oscar Wilde say?" wondered Ari. "A plan that isn't dangerous isn't a plan at all."

"Ah, poor Oscar!" lamented Sir Rennell. "He said *idea*, of course. And I think a large part of his problem was that so many of his ideas were dangerous without being particularly useful."

Preparations took another day, and it was early April when a host of mechanics hauled on the hawser lines of the LS3 and towed her out from under the canopy and into the fresh air. I was with Sikorsky in the wheelhouse. Fritz's voice came through the speaking tube: "The tail the canopy has cleared, Herr McCracken."

He was stationed at the very stern of the airship, on the scaffolding that provided access to the stern engines.

"All right, Fritz," I answered him. "Crank those engines up and get back inside."

One by one, we heard the four Mercedes engines roar and settle down to a hum. Leaning out of the starboard window, I motioned to the ground crew to release the hawsers. The LS3 jolted ever so slightly, then began to rise and inch forward. Sikorsky turned the wheel slightly—it looked like a ship's helm—and pulled back on the yoke. The flaps rose and the LS3's nose lifted. I held on to the wall and glanced back along the length of the airship—I had forgotten how steeply she rose at takeoff.

The pitch of the engines rose as Sikorsky increased the throttle, and the LS3 climbed away from the aerodrome, away from Varese and the little house rented by Vickers-Armstrong. Ahead of us, blue mountains fringed the horizon: the Alps. I watched as our shadow slid over houses and streets, then villas and groves. I gave a little sigh. "Goodbye, Aunt Polly. I'll see you after the War."

But Sikorsky wore a troubled expression, and he pressed the wheel and yoke back and forth a few times. "McCracken," he said, "controls will not respond as normal. We have problem."

"What sort of a problem?" Stepping across to Sikorsky, I touched the wheel and then the yoke. "They don't seem sluggish to me."

Sikorsky looked uneasy. "I fly LS3 with many different payloads. I know how ship feels through wheel and yoke. When we load supplies, I make careful notes. I know current payload. LS3 is heavier than she should be."

"By how much?"

"Three hundred pounds, maybe four hundred.

I frowned. "That could make a difference when we're so short of fuel."

"Herr McCracken." We both spun round in surprise to find that Fritz stood in the doorway. Behind him, in the passageway between the radio and navigation rooms, lurked the enormous bulk of Cadwallader Grubworthy.

Sikorsky gave a grunt. "Three hundred, seventy-eight pounds."

Fritz jabbed a thumb over his shoulder. "Him I find hiding in the food storage compartment."

"Storage compartment?"

"*Jawohl*, Herr McCracken. The food storage compartment. It is large."

I directed my stare at Grubworthy. "A stowaway?"

Grubworthy shouldered past Fritz and into the wheelhouse. "I couldn't stay with that woman any longer," he whined. Dropping his voice confidentially, he said, "I think she was trying to kill me."

"To kill you?"

"By starving me to death! Why else would she dismiss Raimondo? I didn't have any other options. A person of my stature has certain needs."

"You mean quantities of food?"

"Of course not! Well, yes, that did figure into my calculations, of course. I seem to be fated by heaven to need fine foods. It's heaven, not my desire. If it were merely my desire, why I couldn't give a fig for a whole plate of sausages. But the heavens require it of me. It's my destiny. It's my vocation!"

I took a step closer to him. "Grubworthy," I said with menace, "do you know where we're going?"

"Back to England?" He sounded hopeful.

I shook my head. "Germany."

"Oh. That certainly puts a different light on things." His expression brightened. "But perhaps you could make a quick detour?" he suggested.

I shook my head again. "No, Grubworthy. You're in it until the end now."

Grubworthy thought about it for a moment. "Well, let's look on the bright side—weiner schnitzel, pretzels, bratwurst. Germany is not without its merits."

"They're our enemy, Grubworthy. If they catch us, they'll shoot us. Hands behind the back, firing squad, blindfold, the lot."

"They would never shoot me." Grubworthy shook his head in disbelief. His jowls quivered like a plate of jelly on a badly-oiled conveyor belt. "Think how much earth they'd have to shovel out to bury me. It's far too much trouble."

I gave a sigh of resignation. "Well, perhaps you can make yourself useful."

A broad grin split Grubworthy's spherical face. "I could help out in the galley," he offered.

Of course, I didn't let him, though somehow, whenever he helped with any task, be it in the workshop, wheelhouse, carriage house or wherever, he always seemed to end up in the galley or dining room, or at least in some kind of proximity to food.

Meanwhile, the search for Lenin's train began. We couldn't intercept it over Switzerland, because that would violate their neutrality in the War. We knew he would have to change trains at the border. The logical route from there was through Frankfurt and Berlin. But would he attempt to go by a more circuitous route to evade pursuers? Sikorsky flew us north across Switzerland to its border with Germany, a trip of about three hours.

"We should find place to land," suggested Sikorsky, "to preserve fuel."

"Finding a flat spot is going to be tricky," I pointed out, redirecting Archie away from an exit hatch.

At that point, Ari poked her head out of the radio room and called to us in the wheelhouse: "Message from Sir Rennell. Lenin has left Zurich. He's going to change trains at Schaffhausen, then head north to Frankfurt, as we guessed."

"Schaffhausen." Sikorsky and I pored over the large-scale map on the table at the back of the wheelhouse. Grinning, Sikorsky made the Sign of the Cross. "Thank God," he said. "It is very close. Lenin will be here in less than one hour. Where is best place to catch him?"

A sigh came from the doorway, and turning we saw that Grubworthy stood there. "I had to fasten my belt a notch tighter this morning," he lamented. "I believe I'm wasting away to nothing."

"Nothing to worry about," returned Sikorsky. "That will take very long time."

"I knew her ladyship would have this effect on me," Grubworthy went on. He belched. "Oh, these pickled herrings! Not good for my digestion."

"Don't eat them." I turned back to the map. "Perhaps here?" I said to Sikorsky, pressing my finger-tip against the map at a relatively straight length of railway that extended eight or so miles.

"I always make it a point to eat what's placed in front of me," Grubworthy explained. "I could be fussy about what I eat, what with my health and all. In fact, my health really requires that I be most careful what I eat. But I don't want to be any trouble, so I eat whatever they set before me. It's a sacrifice, but worth it. It's just a virtue of mine—that and my honesty."

"We should follow railway at half speed," advised Sikorsky. "Let Lenin catch up with us."

"We only have this chance," I said. "The train can go much faster than we can."

"True," admitted Sikorsky, "but it cannot go in straight line."

"I think, though," said Grubworthy, "her ladyship's loss of chef will prove to have had a permanent effect on my health." He plucked at his jacket. "My clothes are loose on me."

"You sound like Falstaff," Ari observed, sliding past him to enter the wheelhouse. At Grubworthy's puzzled expression, she explained, "You know, in Shakespeare's plays. Falstaff, the fat knight. He says,

'Do I not dwindle? My skin hangs upon me like an old lady's loose gown.'"

Grubworthy nodded thoughtfully. "There is something Falstaffian about me," he agreed, patting his stomach. "I think it's the sharpness of my wit."

"Or the length of your belt," I suggested quietly.

"Well, that too, I suppose," answered Grubworthy. "But when I have been praised—which is not so seldom as you may suppose—it has often been for my wit or my honesty. Many have also praised my humility—rightly, when you consider it."

"We need a spotter astern," I suggested. "I'll watch out of the stern windows in the dining room. Then we can see Lenin's train approaching."

"The dining room?" Grubworthy became suddenly animated. "I can help you there."

I didn't reply. While Ari took a yelling and kicking Archie for his nap, Sikorsky returned to the wheel, turning it hard a-port. The airship started cruising westwards along the Swiss border.

It was not long after that Schaffhausen appeared in our forward windows. It was a beautiful little town near some spectacular waterfalls, surrounded by forests and vineyards. We quickly located the railway station. The tracks cut through the landscape into the north, into Germany.

Sikorsky cut the speed of the LS3 and turned north to follow the railway lines. I headed back towards the dining room, trailing Grubworthy behind me. The view through those panoramic windows was magnificent—a lush valley with mountains above, the Rhine idling along the bottom. Grubworthy poured himself a large glass of port, then rifled through the icebox behind the bar and found some canapés. "I don't think anybody wants these," he muttered to himself. "I'll just finish them off and make some more space in here."

Usually the LS3 moves fairly fast. We almost always have to be somewhere in a hurry. But that day, letting Lenin's train catch us up, we idled along. I watched the lovely scenery of southern Germany unfold beneath us, wondering when the last British eyes had gazed upon those green slopes and picturesque villages. Having lulled Archie to sleep, Ari joined me at the observation window.

"Beautiful," she remarked.

"I should say so!" enthused Grubworthy. "Fritz is a veritable artist with canapés. Have you tried one of these polenta and prosciutto chips?" He held out some golden polenta wrapped around with a shiny slice of prosciutto. I reached out for it, but he withdrew his hand. "I think this is the last one," he said, popping it into his mouth.

With a sigh, I turned back to the observation window.

Behind us, on the tracks, a puff of smoke rose into the sky. I leaped to my feet. Beneath the dissipating smoke, I could see the glossy black barrel of a locomotive train—and we knew that the track had been cleared all the way to Frankfurt. There was only one train that could be. I crossed the dining room in two strides and picked up the speaking tube from behind the bar.

"Sikorsky," I said, "here he comes!"

CHAPTER 6
THE COMMUNIST

I walked briskly out of the dining room to the exit hatch on the port side of the gondola. Glancing through the window beside the hatch, I could see that the train, still a little behind, was slowly gaining on us. It was a bonny little thing, with a lantern on each side of the smoke box and a glossy green boiler. The pistons pounded away madly at the bright scarlet wheels. It was a Borsig, I thought, an 0-2-0 with its wheels spaced quite far apart to give it better balance. Perfect for a winding local route and a relatively small cargo. Lenin would probably have to change trains upon reaching Frankfurt.

I pulled open the exit hatch, and immediately wind roared into the passageway. Ari held her hair out of her face as she kissed me and yelled over the noise of the 84-horsepower Mercedes engines. "God be with you, love!"

"Mmm-hmm," said Grubworthy, waving goodbye with a canapé.

Making the Sign of the Cross, I swung out through the door and began to descend the rope ladder. The wind buffeted me, and I rocked a little and swayed, like a marionette in a wind tunnel. Behind me, the shrill whistle of the engine blasted through the air. It shocked me—the train had gained on us in the short time that had passed since I last looked.

Trees flashed past on either side, while the mountains marched past at a stately pace. Ahead, the track bent a little, and Sikorsky guided the LS3 smoothly through the turn. I lowered myself to the next rung. The ladder whipped back and forth so violently that I couldn't immediately find the rung with my foot, and my progress was slow. Down I went, rung after arduous rung. Above me, I could see Ari's anxious face staring down at me.

No bridges or tunnels, Lord, I prayed.

The engine's whistle tooted one more time, from right beside me. The engineer, I saw, leaned out of the cab door, his eyes wide to see me dangling beside him. I grinned at him and waved cheerily. Puzzled, he returned my wave. I descended a couple more rungs. The roof of the coach lay below me, smooth and grey and punctuated by little ventilators. On either side, a steel railing ran from one end of the coach to the other. I hung just a few feet above the roof now. Taking a deep breath, as if I were jumping into cold waters, I counted to three and dropped.

Jumping onto a moving object isn't easy, and I lost my balance at once, rolling towards the edge. Fortunately, I was able to grasp the steel railing and steady myself. Overhead, the LS3 rose over the train and fell in behind it. I was alone.

My mission was to uncouple the passenger coach. I would get Lenin off the train—I had my revolver to help persuade him—and get him to the LS3. We would then fly north to the German coast and across the North Sea to England, where Lenin would be detained for the duration of the War. I pushed myself to my feet. The coach swayed and rattled beneath me, and I had to hold out my hands for balance.

A voice called out from the front of the coach. I was so surprised I almost fell off. At the front end, I could see Von Krems' face.

"*Kommen du her!*" he shouted, cupping his hands to be heard. "*Kommen du her!*" he repeated, seeing I had not moved.

I was paralyzed. I had no idea what to do. What he was saying sounded like *Come here*. But why would an Austrian, one of our enemies, want me to approach him? Why not just shoot me?

But Von Krems beckoned. "*Was willst du?*" he demanded.

What did he mean? I began to panic. How would Ari have figured it out? *Was willst du?* What will you? What do you want?

Suddenly, I understood what was happening. Everyone on the train had seen the Maltese Crosses on the flanks of the LS3, and assumed I was German.

Von Krems clearly believed me to be his ally, and thought I had boarded with some kind of special message for him or Lenin.

I nodded and held up a hand to indicate that he should be patient. Slowly, I began to move towards the front of the coach. I looked over my shoulder. The LS3 was just a dark disc against the blue of the sky.

At the end of the coach was a ladder, leading down to a small fenced platform. To left and right were steps by which passengers descended to the train platform. A door with a small window in it led into the carriage; opposite was the coal box of the engine. Climbing down, I surreptitiously glanced at the deck of the platform. The coach was coupled to the engine with a Scharfenberg coupler, released by a lever on the underside. But before I could uncouple it, I had to deal with Von Krems.

"*Was willst du?*" he asked again.

He was probably asking what I wanted. I could work out that much. But I couldn't say anything in reply—I could not speak German, or any other language for that matter, and as soon as I opened my mouth, the game would be up.

"*Was is los mit dir?*" demanded Von Krems, impatience creeping into his voice and a furrow appearing between his brows. "*Bist du taub?*"

I shook my head. There was only one way to shut him up. I pointed to something over his left shoulder, and while he was looking away, I cranked my arm back and punched him as hard as I could in the stomach. With a bellow of pain, he doubled up and staggered back a step. All I had to do was step forward and give him a little push.

But before I could finish the job, the door to the interior of the coach opened. For a moment, I saw Von Krems' face, his eyes wide, framed in the door's window; then he was gone, with a cry of pain that was instantly silenced.

Rabotnik had opened the door. He didn't even notice that he'd knocked the Austrian officer off the train. He spent maybe a second assessing the situation, then grabbed the front of my shirt and hauled me off my feet. For a moment I dangled, my feet kicking at nothing. The ugly man's expression was puzzled as he studied me closely. Then he shook me so that my bones rattled against each other. My revolver was shaken out of my pocket, hit the deck of the coach, and spun out into mid-air. Then Rabotnik tossed me through the door like a rag-doll from a catapult. I hit the floor and rolled to a stop in a muddle of arms and legs.

The compartment was a dining coach, with a small bar and neat tables arranged along the sides. It was full of cigarette smoke and people staring curiously at me.

Rabotnik re-entered the coach and shut the door behind him. The noise and the wind died instantly, and all I could hear was the clackety-clack of the wheels rattling over the joints in the tracks.

The door at the opposite end opened, and in came Lenin himself. In the smoke from all the cigarettes, and with his pointy beard, he looked more like Satan than ever. The door clicked softly behind him and there came instantly a flurry of movement from the passengers in the dining coach, stubbing out their cigarettes, throwing them to the ground, waving away smoke to the best of their abilities. Lenin wrinkled his nose in distaste and wafted away smoke with one small hand.

"Who are you?" he asked me in English.

I got to my feet, trembling a little, my body aching where I'd been thrown to the floor. "My name's McCracken."

Lenin nodded knowingly. "An English spy," he said.

"Not English," I retorted angrily, "Scottish."

"But a spy." The communist looked about with curiosity. "Where is Von Krems?"

"He had to get off the train," I told him.

Lenin's eyelids drooped, as if he had heard something bitterly disappointing. "What is the use of getting off the train before you have reached your destination?" he wondered. "It would be like stopping a revolution before killing all your enemies."

I raised an eyebrow. "You must have a lot of enemies," I observed.

"Those who wish to change the world must expect to make enemies." Lenin's lips widened in what would be a smile on any other man's face. "The whole bourgeoisie is my enemy."

"If you want to kill all the ruling classes of the world," I reasoned, "your revolution is going to take a very long time."

The trace of that smile still misted Lenin's lips. "All glorious endeavours take time. Russia is only the beginning. Once we have Russia, we can move on—eastern Europe, western Europe. South America is ripe for revolution. So is Africa. I may not see it in my lifetime, but my successor will see the workers of the world unite and throw off the yoke of bourgeois oppression." One of the smokers, a heavily moustachioed man with features a bit like a rat's who had curiously enough not stubbed out his cigarette, gave a chortle of laughter. "You agree with me, Josef?"

"Of course, Comrade Lenin," answered Josef. He drew a deep lungful of smoke then stubbed out his cigarette.

Lenin took a step closer to me. "Who are you?" he demanded.

"My name is McCracken," I said. "That's all you'll get."

Josef cleared his throat and beckoned Lenin over to him. He whispered in his ear. Lenin looked over at me, then back at Josef. Eventually, he returned and sized me up. "You are the McCracken who killed Baron Hohenstaufen? Who defeated Professor Lychfield? The bandit Calavera? And Captain Strombourg of the French Navy?"

I grinned. "I'm glad you've heard of me."

"And you think I don't know why you're here?" Lenin growled like an animal. "You Catholics disgust me. Every religious idea, every idea of God, it is unutterable vileness. It is filth of the most dangerous, of the most abominable type. What is your religion but opium for the masses? Faced with their powerlessness in the capitalist society, what can they do but benumb their misery in a foolish belief in a better life after death? To any enlightened individual it is not only a right but a duty to destroy religion in all its forms, but the Catholic Church most of all. No organization in history has more successfully suppressed the workers than your Church. Its existence alone justifies violent revolution."

"Well, that's an interesting opinion."

In a sudden, vicious move, Lenin slapped me across the face, and I sprawled on the floor. "That is no opinion!" he raged. "That is fact! You will not get the Kazanskaya! You will not get it, do you understand? We will get it and we will destroy it, and that terrible woman will not protect Russia from our revolution!"

"What is the Kazanskaya?" I asked innocently.

"Miserable lying dog," snarled Lenin. "Capitalist pig! Filthy little Catholic spy!" He suddenly smiled. "You know, do you not, what happens to spies, when we find them?"

"You shoot them?"

Lenin shook his head. "No, comrade," he said. "We let them run for their lives." Stepping past me, he turned the handle and opened the door to the outside. I could see the engine, I could smell the smoke, I could feel the wind blowing into the coach.

Rabotnik took my arm and pushed me towards the door. He grinned. Reaching into his pocket, he drew out a shining black cannonball.

CHAPTER 7
THE LOST LADY OF KAZAN

Rabotnik did not take his eyes from me. He merely stepped aside to allow me through the door. He tossed the cannonball a couple of inches from his hand and caught it again, over and over. My mind raced. What was this Kazanskaya? How could I get out of the range of Rabotnik's cannonballs? Were they going to push me from the train? Kill me at close quarters? I prayed for help from Our Lady.

With his free hand, Rabotnik pressed down on the heavy handle of the door and pushed it open. The sound of the engine and the smell of the smoke gusted into the coach. I could see the near end of the tender jolting over the rails ahead of us. Rabotnik nodded his head towards the door. I took a step forward.

A calmness settled over me. I've found this in dangerous situations before. It's as if time slows down. I become more aware of my surroundings, of details I hadn't seen before. I noticed, for example, a little shape tattooed onto Rabotnik's neck: a Russian Orthodox Crucifix, with the three crossbeams that look so odd to western eyes.

I also saw the emergency brake chain, right beside the door, and as I passed through, I reached up and yanked down hard on it.

At once the emergency brakes squealed and the whole carriage lurched into the tender, sending every loose object flying. Rabotnik lost his balance and tumbled through the door, while Lenin was pitched to the floor, cursing loudly in Russian. Screams and shouts erupted from all around us. I held onto the chain, flattened against the wall for a moment, while chaos raged.

The instant order began to return, I leaped through the door, shoving Rabotnik aside. The train had slowed almost to a stop, and I dropped down through the gap between the tender and the carriage, swinging my feet up and looping them over some of the struts underneath the carriage. The wooden sleepers flashed by underneath me, but slower as the train decreased speed. Reaching up, I pulled down on the coupling lever. I felt a jolt as the two halves of the coupling separated. Then, tucking my elbows in and my knees together, I let go of the underneath of the carriage. I landed with a thud and a grunt beneath the train and between the steel rails. Wheels rolled by on either side of me. Axle after axle rumbled past overhead. I kept as still as I could and prayed for my safety.

Daylight showed above me. I sprang to my feet and dived into the ditch at the side of the railway lines.

Instantly, a soft thud came from the earth beside my ear and I saw half a cannonball protruding from the embankment. My eyes wide, I turned to look along the slowing train. There was Rabotnik, hanging from the railing on the side of the carriage. The motion of the train had thrown off his aim, but he was still disturbingly close. I picked myself up and dashed away from the railway lines and into some undergrowth.

There wasn't much noise from the train by now, except for the hissing of steam, but I could hear a buzzing overhead and recognized the LS3's Mercedes engines. The rope ladder formed a ruler-straight line, at the bottom of which Cadwallader Grubworthy swung like the pendulum of a grandfather clock. He dropped to the ground with a sound like air being punched out of a balloon, rolled, and scrambled to join me.

"I've been sent to fetch you, Crackers," he said.

"McCracken," I corrected him.

Grubworthy nodded. "They said we'd eat lunch early if I came after you. I have a gun." He tossed it to me before I could stop him and it went off as it struck my hand. The bullet whizzed past Grubworthy's forehead and smacked into the railway line with a *ding!*

"Grubworthy, always put the safety catch on when you're carrying a gun!" I shouted. "Have some respect for firearms!"

"Sorry, I've never carried one before."

The train, meanwhile, had come to a stop, and people were jumping down from the carriage. I couldn't see Rabotnik among them, and wondered where he was. Was he in the undergrowth too, stalking us as a man with a shotgun hunts pheasants?

The engine and the carriages, I noticed, had not separated as I had hoped. If all had gone according to plan, the engine would have pulled away as the uncoupled carriages had lost momentum. But with the engine decelerating, the carriages' momentum had actually pressed them against the tender. They were uncoupled but still together. It wouldn't take the engineer long to recouple and move off.

We didn't have much time, but at least I had a gun and Grubworthy. I looked up at the LS3. The underside of the gondola was utterly featureless from this perspective, and the envelope seemed to stretch out infinitely. Crossing cautiously to the other side of the tracks, I crept along the embankment towards the train.

Lenin, red-faced, was arguing with the engineer, while a couple of people held guns and scanned this way and that with their eyes. They watched the LS3 keenly, and one of them raised a rifle to his shoulder. A shot barked out, but the bullet pinged harmlessly from the LS3's metal skin. Another of the guards reached out to press down the muzzle of his gun; he knew as I did that ordinary bullets couldn't do any damage to an airship. British fighters over London had to combine explosive with incendiary bullets in order to pierce the skin of a zeppelin, ignite the hydrogen inside and bring it down. And we had an extra layer of a special kind of fabric that I'd picked up in Asia a couple of years previously that was bullet-proof and heat resistant. The LS3 was in no danger.

I spoke to Grubworthy without turning around, explaining to him a plan by which he could distract the guards while I overpowered Lenin and dragged him to the LS3. "It's just Rabotnik that worries me," I concluded. "Where is he?" Grubworthy said nothing. I glanced back at him, over my shoulder.

He was nowhere to be seen.

At that moment, the train whistle blew and the engine let off a huge cloud of steam. The engineer disengaged from his argument with Lenin and climbed into the cab. The passengers started climbing back up into the coaches.

The moment was disappearing. I looked up longingly at the LS3. We had an airship! Why couldn't we do anything about this?

Where on earth was Grubworthy? I crept stealthily back a few paces, and there he was, still on the far side of the tracks, quietly waiting. He hadn't moved an inch since hiding in the embankment. I beckoned for him to join me, but he wasn't looking. Cupping my hands about my mouth, I yelled out his name. He heard me, rose in a leisurely fashion, and started walking towards me.

"Quicker, Grubworthy!" I shouted. He began shambling, barely faster than he had been walking.

Suddenly, with a yelp like a kicked dog, Grubworthy flung out his arms and pitched forward into the long grass, where he lay still. Only his backside rose, like a hill, above the grass. Behind him stood Rabotnik. The huge Russian saw me and began running towards the still form of Grubworthy.

"Rabotnik!" came the shrill scream of Lenin, from the train, and the big man slowed to a stop. He and I stood silently, the body of Grubworthy lying prone between us.

"Rabotnik!" yelled Lenin again. He added something in Russian, which sounded very angry.

Rabotnik took two steps forward, stooped, picked up the cannonball that had hit Grubworthy, and ran off along the tracks towards the departing train. Hands at the rear of the train reached out, took him, and lifted him into the coach as it began to pick up speed.

We had lost Lenin. We had lost Grubworthy. I sank to my knees beside the stowaway and felt tears welling up behind my eyes. I had not liked him, and now I had no chance to change my mind about him.

But then Grubworthy groaned. His hand fluttered up and clutched his backside. "Owww!" he lamented. "Owww!"

"Grubworthy, you're alive!" I cried, leaping towards him. "I thought Rabotnik had killed you for sure with than cannonball!" Grubworthy rolled over, but lying on his back evidently gave him great pain. "Where did he get you?" I asked in wonder.

Grubworthy gave a low moan. "A gentleman," he said, "doesn't talk about such things." He rubbed his backside tenderly. "But I think I should add that possessing a body that absorbs a certain amount of violent impact can be a considerable advantage at times."

I would have laughed, but at that moment the engine's whistle sounded, and the train carrying Lenin sped off, now well out of reach.

I helped Grubworthy to his feet—no easy task—and together we found the LS3's rope ladder. Once inside the airship, Grubworthy raced off to his cabin to nurse his sore backside, while I found Ari in the passageway outside the dining room, Archie at her heels. Archie held out to me something in his clenched hand. "Candy," he said.

"Thank you." I reached out to take a piece, but then realized he was describing it, not offering it. I turned to Ari. "Why didn't you come to help me? Why send Grubworthy? He was useless. We lost Lenin."

"Archie woke up." Stepping closer, Ari added in a low voice, "Did you want me to leave him with Cadwallader?"

I glanced back along the passageway in the rough direction of Grubworthy's cabin. "I suppose not."

"Lenin escaped?" Sikorsky had joined us from the wheelhouse, having left Fritz at the helm. I nodded disconsolately. "Is too bad."

"What is a Kazanskaya?" I asked.

"Kazanskaya!" I was taken aback by Sikorsky's reaction. His eyes widened and he took a step backwards, as if he had been hit in the chest. "Where is it you hear of this thing?"

"Lenin mentioned it. He seemed to think I wanted it, but he said I wouldn't get it. He said he was going to destroy it."

Sikorsky leaned on the sill of one of the portholes, and watched the luscious German landscape rolling by below us. Ari and I exchanged glances. Archie finished his sweet and held out his arms to be picked up. I hoisted him into my arms, and found his hands to be sticky. I carried him behind the bar and washed him off in the sink. "Sikorsky?" I said, noticing that no one had accompanied me.

Sikorsky, like a man in a dream, entered the dining room, Ari behind him. "Of course Lenin would want to destroy Kazanskaya. For almost five hundred years, she has protected Russia, but he thinks only he should protect Russia."

"She?" said Ari. "This Kazanskaya is a woman?"

"Of course she is woman!" Sikorsky seemed surprised at our dullness. "She is *the* woman, the Virgin of Kazan!"

"Our Lady?" said Ari.

Sikorsky nodded. "Come. I show you." He led us up the stairs to the second floor of the gondola. At the end of the long central passageway was the library, filled with the volumes we had inherited from the LS3's previous owner. Most of the books were in German, but a fair number were in other languages too.

Sikorsky went straight to the art history section, ran his finger along the spines of a number of books and then drew a large leather-bound volume from the shelf. The title was written in gold-leaf in the beautiful Cyrillic lettering of the Russian language. Placing the book carefully on the desk, he consulted the index, then turned a few thick pages until he found what he was looking for. It was a print of a picture of Mary and Jesus that looked medieval to me. Jesus looked less like a baby than a miniature adult. It was covered with a thin translucent page, which Sikorsky moved aside.

"This is lost Lady of Kazan. That is what *Kazan-skaya* means: Virgin of Kazan. Kazan is city far east of Moscow. Kazanskaya is holy icon, maybe this big." He held his hands about two feet apart horizontally, then three vertically. "She shows the Holy Mother and the Child."

"So it's a picture of the Virgin Mary and Jesus?" I said.

Sikorsky gave a frustrated gasp, and for the first time, as I watched him, I wished I could speak Russian. He said, "Icon is not just picture. Is icon—is a window through which we see God."

"Sounds like magic to me."

"No!" Sikorsky wagged his forefinger at me. "Is wrong to speak this way of Our Mother of Kazan. You do not understand holy icons in Russian Orthodox Church. Icon is very important thing. When icon is made, is not painted—is *written*. Icon has meaning in it, and only the holiest of meanings. You look at icon, you see truth. You see God."

I realized I had just committed a minor infraction of politeness with regard to this artwork, and so said nothing more, but just let Sikorsky continue.

"Virgin of Kazan is old, very old—perhaps a thousand years old. She was lost for many years, but Our Lady came to small child in Kazan, a twelve-year-old girl name Marfa Onuchin, and showed her where it was." He paused, searching for a way of expressing in English the deeply Russian thoughts that were rushing through his mind. "I am not Orthodox, McCracken. I am not Russian. I am Ukrainian, and that means I am Catholic, like many of my countrymen, but Eastern Rite. And Eastern Rite is closer to Orthodox than Roman Rite. We think like Orthodox. We feel like Orthodox. An icon is more than a picture; is a sacramental, almost a relic. When we venerate icon, we venerate God *through* icon. Is how we love God. And He loves us through icon also. Many times, when Russia is invaded, army carries Virgin of Kazan into battle, and each time Russia is victorious! If Bolsheviks destroy icon, it will be nothing but man against man when Russia is invaded—God will not help us." He shook his head slowly. "Is not magic. Icon does not change rules of nature. Icon is window through which we look at God, and He looks at us. Is one of the ways God loves us."

"Surely it will be easy enough to protect the icon against Lenin," I reasoned. "We jut have to alert the authorities in this city of Kazan. If they know he's after it, and wants to destroy it, surely they'll protect it from him."

"Perhaps they would," replied Sikorsky, "if they knew where is Lady. But where is she? Where is Virgin of Kazan? Ten years ago, she was stolen by thieves. They wanted frame—it has gold and many jewels in it—and threw away icon itself. No one knows where icon is—or no one knows until now. It seems that Vladimir Ilyich Lenin knows, and will stop at nothing to destroy icon so he can rule Russia as sole protector."

"That settles it," I said. "Now we *have* to catch Lenin."

"*Nyet!*" said Sikorsky with vehemence. He shook his head. "Lenin unimportant—Lady of Kazan is all now. We must find Lady of Kazan."

"But if we follow Lenin, he'll lead us to the icon," I said.

"Perhaps," replied Sikorsky, "or perhaps he will send another after icon. But quickest way to defeat Lenin is find icon and give her to Imperial Russian Army."

"Is there an Imperial Russian Army any more?" I wondered.

"Is true," admitted Sikorsky. "Now Tsar Nikolai is gone, to whom do we give her?"

No one spoke for a while. Archie started wriggling and making a noise like a rusty hinge. "Use your words," I told him.

"Dah," he said, and I set him down on the floor. He toddled over to lean on the window, where he left two tiny handprints on the glass. Ari picked him up and sat down with him at the desk, studying the print of the icon and preventing Archie from touching it.

"So, what do we do?" I asked. "Do we follow Lenin or go after the Lady of Kazan?"

Sikorsky looked helpless. "I cannot tell," he said.

"Is there really a choice?" Ari looked up from studying the print. "Mac, who wants you to follow Lenin?"

"Sir Rennell," I answered. "The British Government. That's a pretty high authority."

"And who wants you to go after the Kazanskaya?"

"Well," I began, and paused. Suddenly, it was all clear to me. "An even higher authority than His Majesty's Government," I concluded. Ari smiled. I reached for the speaking tube by the door and blew into it.

"Herr McCracken?" came Fritz's voice.

"A new heading, Fritz," I said. "Due east."

"Herr McCracken?"

"Due east, Fritz," I repeated. "We're going to Russia."

Chapter 8
A Short Detour

Unfortunately, my optimism was premature. We couldn't fly due east, as that would take us directly over the Eastern Front, and into a war zone. War raged all the way from the Baltic to the Black Sea. Instead, we had to turn south-east, heading for the Adriatic. That took us over the Alps, and we climbed over the peaks, gleaming blue in the moonlight, and descended when the sun was rising.

We had missed Grubworthy at supper, which surprised us all a great deal, but he appeared once more at breakfast, as Fritz dished up cheese, sausage and bread rolls fresh from the oven. He very ginger-ly lowered himself into a seat across the table from us, with a sharp intake of breath as he touched the leather.

Archie gave a giggle and turning to him Grub-worthy said, "I don't think you understand at all how I suffer."

"I fufuff," said Archie in sympathy.

Helping himself to a mound of food, Grubwor-thy glanced curiously out of the window. The rich landscape of northern Italy lay spread out below us. "Are we in England already?" he asked, munching on some sausage.

"Ingle ready," repeated Archie, in a sing-song voice.

"That's Italy," I observed.

Grubworthy's eyes widened. "Are we returning to her ladyship?" he asked in a tremulous voice.

"We're on our way to Russia," Ari explained.

"Oh, thank goodness!" Grubworthy recommenced shoveling sausages into his mouth. "Why Russia?" he asked after a moment.

"We missed Lenin in Germany." My tone probably conveyed my irritation with him, but he didn't appear to notice. "We have to go to Russia to defeat him there."

"Defeat Lenin?" Grubworthy sounded alarmed.

"Feety Lenny. Lenny feet," chimed in Archie.

I explained the situation to Grubworthy. He gave a sigh. "I had thought we would return to England."

"Turny Inglie," agreed Archie solemnly. Grubworthy turned a venomous eye on him. Archie beat on the table a few times with his spoon.

Grubworthy ate slowly and in a preoccupied manner. After a few moments, he said, "Isn't Russia a frightfully cold place?"

"It'll be getting warmer when we get there," Ari told him.

"Hm." Grubworthy didn't sound convinced.

Fritz heaped more sausage and cheese on the table. He glanced at Grubworthy sidelong, and then at me. He said, "I am glad, Herr McCracken, that we to Russia shall travel. It will give me the chance to learn how to make Paskha."

Grubworthy raised an inquisitive eyebrow. "What, pray, is Paskha?"

Fritz gave a nonchalant shrug. "It is a kind of confection the Russians eat at Easter. Only in rumours have I heard of it, Herr Grubworthy."

"Hm. Is Easter gone by now?" asked Grubworthy.

"Almost a month ago, Cadwallader," said Ari, her lip twisting in a disapproving manner.

Leaning close, Fritz said to Grubworthy in a confidential manner, "They sake Paskha has sixty eggs in it and over thirteen pounds of sugar."

"No!" breathed Grubworthy. "Fritz, that's almost indecent."

"*Ja*, that is what I have heard. *Unt* there is a great deal of fruit in it: raisins and candied fruit and so forth. It is the kind of cake that on the large Russian estates they eat. We could perhaps a portion of that recipe make."

Grubworthy sliced a bread roll in half and admired how the butter melted into it for a moment. "Well, Fritz, let's not make a hasty judgment about that. Perhaps we should make the recipe entire. We wouldn't want to spoil it, you know." Half the bread roll vanished into his mouth and after swallowing he concluded, "Well, perhaps Russia has something to offer, after all."

In the late morning, we began our descent towards Venice. We had cabled Sir Rennell, and he had suggested we land at the San Nicolò Aerodrome, which was situated on the Lido, the long thin island that guarded the lagoon on which Venice was built. A squadron of fighters of the *Corpo Aeronautico Militare*, the Italian Air Force, was stationed there, and Sir Rennell thought we might be able to pick up more fuel there. He had also asked me to call him by telephone once we had landed.

"They probably have a telephone at the aerodrome," remarked Ari, showing me the transcript of Sir Rennell's message in the wheelhouse. She peered past me and out of the window. "Are those aeroplanes?" she asked, pointing.

Two shapes were moving towards us, which quickly resolved themselves into the double wings of a pair of Nieuport 11s bearing the red, white and green roundels of the *Corpo Aeronautico*.

"Perhaps they want to escort us to the aerodrome," I suggested.

Sikorsky, who was manning the helm, cried out: "Hit deck!" and pushed Ari to the floor. A second later, something punched holes in the steel walls of the wheelhouse and shattered the glass in the windows. Shards of glass tinkled about me.

"What on earth are they doing?" I heard the engines of the planes speeding by beneath us.

"This is ridiculous," said Ari. "Archie's sleeping."

Sikorsky said something angry in Russian and slapped his forehead. "Still we have crosses painted on sides. They think we are German."

"Here they come again!" Ari dived to the floor as bullets tore through the wheelhouse, this time from the starboard side. I started praying Hail Marys.

"Ha!" cried Sikorsky, as the planes flew off on the port side and began their long turn to begin a new attack run. "Their bullets cannot pierce our envelope! Ha!"

"At the moment," I said, "I'm worried about us in here." I looked around. "Where's Ari?" I asked. I crawled to the port side of the wheelhouse and peered through the window. Freezing air billowed through it. The Italian planes were just coming out of their turn and beginning their strafing run. "Have they wondered why we haven't returned fire yet?" I asked of no one in particular.

I heard a movement behind me, and in a moment Ari stood beside me. She held something black and mechanical in her hands, and I recognized the portable Aldiss Lamp we kept in the radio room for signaling in Morse Code. She flipped the switch and snapped the shutter open and closed rapidly.

"What are you saying to them?" I asked. "Please stop shooting, we're on your side?"

"They wouldn't believe that." Open, shut, open, shut.

The planes were close now. I could see the pilots' faces, wrapped in scarves and goggles and leather helmets. Any moment now they would open up.

Snap-snap-snappity-snap went the shutter of the Aldiss Lamp. I could see the light going on and off, reflected in the shards of glass framing the open window.

The planes closed in. My fingers tensed about an upright strut and I ducked below the window, bracing myself for the bullets to rip through the steel shell of the gondola.

But mercifully, they did not open fire. I heard the engines roar below us, and slowly stood to watch them fly away from us and bank slowly to the port to race on ahead of us a little way. Then they turned slowly and returned. Ari pointed the Aldiss Lamp towards them and flashed her message to them one more time. Closer and closer the planes flew. Then, just when it seemed they would collide with us, the Nieuports parted and rushed by us, one on either side of the gondola. One of them waggled his wings up and down. Then they peeled off and flew into the south.

"What did you say to them?" I asked Ari again.

"*Ti voglio bene,*" she replied. "It means 'I love you,'" but between good friends. It's more like, 'I wish you well.' No German would think of saying that."

"Bravo, madam!" cried Sikorsky. "Is well done." He returned to his position behind the helm.

Grubworthy stood in the doorway, a sandwich in one hand. "Has there been some trouble?" he asked. "I thought I heard some noises from the galley."

"Is more trouble than I thought," said Sikorsky. He pushed one of the spokes of the helm, and it rattled around freely. "The Italian pilots, they have severed the tiller cables. We cannot steer." Reaching for the speaking tube, he called for Fritz, who appeared in a few moments. When we explained the situation to him, Fritz frowned.

"If the wheel does not work," he reasoned, "what good am I?"

"Rudder does not work," answered Sikorsky, "but elevators, they work. You cannot control direction, but you can control altitude." Fritz nodded.

We rattled up the ladders into the crawl-space above the wheelhouse. The wind whistled through half a dozen bullet-holes up there.

Right away, we saw the problem. The tiller cable had been severed about twenty feet from the helm, and lay curled like a snake along the floor. At first, I couldn't see the other end, the end that was attached to the rudder. I found it by crawling aft some distance and shining my electric torch into the darkness. Sikorsky and I heaved on it, but we couldn't pull it even a foot closer to the other end.

"The tiller cable isn't even half an inch in diameter," I said, shouting aboe the rush of the wind in the crawl-space. "What are the chances a bullet would sever it?"

Sikorsky shook his head. "Thousands to one." He waved a hand at the severed cable and the bullet-holes. "All this damage, it will take one week, perhaps two weeks, to repair."

We scrambled back down the ladder and into the wheelhouse. Outside, we could see a gentle countryside, one of wide fields and cypress-lined roads dotted with red-roofed villas.

Sikorsky said something in Russian. He was consulting the compass. Looking up, he explained, "Prevailing wind is from mountains, but it has blown us off-course."

"By much?" I asked.

"*Nyet*," he replied. "But a small amount now is a big difference at end of journey; and we cannot control it."

"Can we land here?" I pointed through the windows.

"*Da*," admitted Sikorsky, dragging the syllable out. "But in field?" He shrugged. "Better in sea. We can ride gondola to aerodrome to get supplies."

"All right then." I rolled my sleeves up. "Let's do what we can."

It was an agonizing flight, not knowing where we were heading, more like flying a hot air balloon than an airship. We seemed to crawl along, and every gust of wind made me frantic. For an hour the journey lasted; then at last we saw a blue line lying along the horizon that widened slowly and became the Adriatic Sea.

Sikorsky pressed gently on the elevator controls and the LS3's nose tipped downwards. For a few moments, the green fields filled our forward vision, then the airship swung upwards once more. We were flying below four hundred feet. Sikorsky cut the speed back to about twenty knots—avoiding obstacles was much more difficult if we could not fly around them but only over them.

Before long we passed over the shining white margin of a beach and cut our engines to drift over the sea. Sikorsky threw a lever, and I heard metallic clanking as the bow anchors dropped. Another lever dropped the stern anchors. When they hit the bottom of the sea, he slowly cranked the cables back in. The LS3 lowered itself towards the gleaming sapphire of the Adriatic Sea until the belly of the gondola touched the wave-tops.

Five or six miles off to the port, we could see the terracotta tiles and white domes of Venice. Out to sea lay a scattering of naval vessels, from dreadnoughts all the way down to torpedo boats. During the War, Venice had been converted into a naval dockyard.

We spent a little while detaching the gondola from the envelope. In an emergency, a single lever could dump the whole thing into whatever lay below, but if we wanted to be careful about it, we had first to detach the wheelhouse from the rest of the gondola and then winch the rest down into the water. The back wall of the library consisted of several panels, which, on being removed, revealed wide windows and a helm. The gondola now resembled a yacht, with the cabins and the new wheelhouse forming the top deck.

It was when we had just lowered the gondola into the water and the sun was lighting the dome of St. Mark's with pink, that Fritz hurried into the library with a message. "Herr McCracken, we have, I think, a visitor."

Looking out of the starboard windows, I saw a Macchi M.5 seaplane had landed not far off and was cutting through the waters towards us.

I immediately left the library and descended the stairs to the hatch on the lower deck. Turning the handle, I pushed it open just as the M.5 came alongside. The pilot cut the engine and threw a line out to us. I caught it and secured it to the gondola. The pilot heaved himself out of the cockpit and walked along the wing to the hatch and then climbed up into the gondola. All this time, he had removed neither his helmet nor his flying goggles. He wore a small triangular beard and a neat moustache. He put his hands on his hips and shook his head sadly.

"I might have known," he said in excellent English with an Italian accent "when I saw that message flashed from the wheelhouse of a zeppelin, that it could only be the McCrackens!"

"Who are you?" I demanded.

"Don't you know?" Ari's voice came from behind me. There she stood, grinning from ear to ear, with Archie on her hip. "How are you doing, Serpe?"

The pilot tore off his helmet and goggles, revealing the dashing face of my old friend from Imperial College and other adventures, Cristofero Campo di Serpenti—Serpe for short.

Serpe had come to apologize for shooting at us, but also with an invitation from his wife, Maria. We were to dine that evening at the Albergo Paradiso, a hotel on the Lido where the officers from all the nearby squadrons ate and slept.

The Albergo Paradiso looked like it was about three hundred years old, with tall windows evenly spaced along its two wings and a grand entrance at the top of wide central steps. Serpe and Maria met us on these steps, and Ari and Maria fell immediately into conversation about God knows what, because I don't speak Italian. Officers were arriving as we climbed the steps, most with Italian girls on their arms. They greeted Serpe in French, and he responded in the same language. The sun was setting as a waiter seated us on a verandah overlooking a lawn, a wide space of ocean, and the skyline of Venice, tinted with pink and purple.

In response to a question from Sikorsky, Serpe said, "I think you will have difficulty finding fuel, Vasili Ivanovich. Fuel is in short supply. You see that gentleman over there." He pointed to a short officer in his mid-fifties with a neat beard and an eye-patch. "That is Gabriele D'Annunzio, who commands the San Marco Bomber Squadron. He also seeks much fuel. He wishes to conduct a raid on Vienna."

"A bombing raid?" I asked.

Serpe shook his head. "He wishes to drop leaflets on Vienna, encouraging the Austrians to surrender. He also wishes for much fuel. D'Annunzio flew the fighters for a time, and that is how he lost his eye. The high command will be more inclined to listen to him than—I crave your pardon, *amico mio*—to civilians."

"I think I'll have the wine-poached salmon with black truffles," Grubworthy said to the waiter. "Oh, and the grilled sole too. Ah, one other thing, Waiter. What is Coquilles Saint-Jacques?" The waiter leaned close and explained something to him *sotto voce*.

Grubworthy beamed with pleasure. "One of those too, I think. Thank you!"

As he handed his menu back to the waiter, a dull thud broke the silence of the darkening sky and the silhouette of Venice was for a moment lit up as if by lightning.

"Is that an air-raid?" I asked.

Serpe nodded sadly. "At least once a week they come, whenever the weather is fine. They bomb the naval ships and the railway yard on the mainland." He swilled his wine around in his glass and took a disconsolate sip. "All the golden angels of Venice wear sackcloth, all the beautiful hotels are turned into hospitals, or quarters for officers, like this one."

"Our mission is important too," I argued, and I told him briefly about our mission to recover the Kazanskaya, with Sikorsky adding details as necessary. When I had finished, I said, "What a coincidence, though, that it should be you flying one of those planes!"

The waiter arrived once more, this time carrying stuffed mushrooms. "Compliments of the chef," he said, "for Signore McCracken."

I frowned. "Actually," I said, "I'm happy with what I've got."

"If you don't want them, I'll take them," said Grubworthy. His hand flashed out and, with a precision I had not suspected in him, speared a mushroom with his fork. The waiter looked alarmed and tried to take the plate away, but Grubworthy wouldn't let him, sweeping the stuffed mushrooms onto his already considerably piled-up plate.

Serpe watched him for a moment in silence. At last, he spoke. "I do not think it is a coincidence, *amico mio.* Does it not seem to you that there is a force far greater than any of us managing events?"

"God?" I said.

Serpe nodded and crossed himself. "This Kazanskaya, she is not like the Mayan treasure we were after the last time we met. That was a petty business, just money for the Germans and a teaching appointment for Professor Lychfield. But this—the Kazanskaya is far greater. She touches two worlds. I feel we are at a fork in the road. Which way will we go? There is the way of the Kazanskaya, the way of God, Truth, and Light; or there is the way of this monster Lenin—the way of the tyrant, of godless government. Which way will the world go?"

"I say," said Grubworthy, burping, "these stuffed mushrooms are very tasty. Are you sure you don't want one, McCracken? No? Never mind—all the more for me."

The following morning, I began to talk to the Italian High Command about requisitioning some fuel. It took me all morning to get to see anyone, and D'Annunzio was there before me. I got referred to someone else, whose offices were in Venice. By the time I returned to the LS3, I was late for lunch, and found Ari and Serpe talking to a stranger in the dining room.

"Mac, this is Dr. Burchiella." We shook hands. "It looks like Cadwallader has gotten food poisoning."

The doctor wagged his finger in correction. "Not bad food, signora," he said. "The symptoms of Signore Grubworthy are of poisoning from belladonna: the sensitivity to light, the dilated pupils, his increased heart-rate, his headache, his loss of balance. My guess would be that someone deliberately tried to poison him."

"Who would do that to poor Cadwallader?" asked Ari in anguish.

"Any offended chef might give it a shot," I pointed out.

"Mac, how can you say such a thing!"

Dr. Burchiella frowned at me. "This is very serious indeed, Signore McCracken. Signore Grubworthy has consumed enough belladonna to kill a man."

I was shocked. "How long has he got?" I asked in a weak voice.

"I will return this evening, and again tomorrow morning," Dr. Burchiella promised, picking up his medical bag. "Keep him warm, keep giving him fluids. If he lasts through the night, there is a chance he may survive."

When he had gone, I turned to Serpe. "Those stuffed mushrooms!" I exclaimed. "Perhaps whoever did it was trying to get me."

"I have started making investigations at the Paradiso," said Serpe. "We will find this would-be assassin today!"

I spent the afternoon trying again to find fuel for the LS3, while Sikorsky worked tirelessly on repairing the damage inflicted by the Italian fighters. When I got back that evening, Grubworthy was in no better a shape, and Ari stayed up all night to make sure he was all right. That meant that every time Archie woke up, I had to change his nappy or rock him back to sleep, and I didn't manage to emerge from my cabin until almost ten o'clock the following morning. I padded along in my dressing gown and slippers to Grubworthy's cabin, knocked and entered.

Ari was sitting in a chair beside the bed, asleep, but the covers of the bed had been tossed aside, and other than the enormous indentation in the mattress, there was no evidence of Grubworthy anywhere.

Ari woke up with a start. "Where's Cadwallader?" she asked.

He wasn't in the dining room, so we checked the galley, and there he was, a plateful of pancakes soaked in syrup before him.

"Grubworthy, you look as right as rain!" I declared.

"I'm feeling much better, thank you," replied Grubworthy, between mouthfuls. "Just a little hungry."

While Ari and I were enjoying our own breakfast in the dining room, Serpe turned up with some news. It turned out that one of the Italian chefs at the Albergo Paradiso had fled without a trace the previous day. The head chef, a Frenchman, had told Serpe he never liked him. "He was a communist," he said with distaste.

That afternoon, while Sikorsky worked on the repairs, I continued my quest for fuel, which took a long time and is difficult to make interesting when it is written down. The fuel we needed certainly existed, but it was accessible only to people who did favours for other people, or who knew what questions to ask in what backrooms.

I was on my way back to the port one afternoon, after about a fortnight of frustrating searching, when I heard a voice calling my name. Turning, I saw a motor launch on the canal beside me, manned by a couple of Italians in dark suits. One of them had removed his jacket to reveal his waistcoat and rolled up sleeves. The other wore his jacket and a wide-brimmed hat, and he sported a thick moustache. Both wore dark glasses.

"Signore McCracken, will you get into the boat, *per favore*?"

I frowned. "Why should I?"

"The man I work for would be very grateful," said Hat.

"Gratitude's a good thing," I answered. "Who do you work for?"

Sleeves sniggered. "I think it would be best if you found out that for yourself. He doesn't want his name thrown around in a public place like this at this time."

My blood ran cold. I looked about for a place I could run, and up ahead saw a bridge, one of the typical hump-backed bridges with a black iron railing you see so often in Venice. But before I could complete an escape plan, Hat had climbed up onto the pavement and drawn a 9mm Glisenti 1910 pistol. "The man I work for," he said, "insists."

So that was it, I thought as I climbed down into the launch. Somehow, we had attracted the attention of . . . what? The Mafia? What on earth could these crime bosses want with me? I wondered as Sleeves throttled the engine and we sped off down the canal, the wind whipping our hair. Hat took off his hat to reveal a bald head fringed by dark hair. He grinned at me and pocketed the gun.

We emerged from the canal and into the open lagoon. Sleeves eased up the speed of the launch so that it bounced over the wave-tops. Ahead of us lay a small island, on which rose a crumbling old mansion that must once have belonged to a wealthy Venetian merchant like Antonio in Shakespeare's play. The sun was beginning to set, and I could see that a single light burned in one of the windows.

We moored our boat at a little jetty, and climbed some rickety steps to a small courtyard, then entered the house. I found myself in a wide hallway with sweeping stairs at one end and doors to left and right. Hat nodded towards the right-hand door, and I walked through it into a room that was furnished with a table, a few chairs, and a solid sideboard that looked as if it were about four hundred years old. On the wall hung a curious painting of the Crucifixion. Skulls were piled around the foot of the cross, and Mary had fainted for grief. I was ordered to sit in one of the chairs, and Sleeves stood guard at the door while Hat went after his boss.

A long time seemed to pass, while I studied the painting, wondering about the skulls. The blood of the Redeemer dripped from His wounds and over the top of the skulls.

The door opened and a man entered. He wasn't who I expected, but I recognized him at once, of course.

"Your Holiness!" I cried, and falling to my knees before him, I kissed the Fisherman's Ring.

CHAPTER 9
TO RUSSIA AT LAST

Giacomo Paolo Giovanni Battista della Chiesa, or His Holiness Pope Benedict XV, was a slender man of about sixty, whose hair was still dark though by now thinning. He seemed to me as one who was weary to the bones, but bore his cross with patience. He placed his hands on the arm-rests of the chair opposite mine and lowered himself into it, motioning me to resume my own seat.

The Pope regarded me with benevolence for a moment, while all I could do was blink in surprise. In slow and deliberate English, he said, "Signore McCracken, please forgive the melodramatic way in which I brought you here." He indicated the world all around. "There are spies everywhere, you see. Everywhere. And for diplomatic reasons, history must record that I am elsewhere at the moment. The Germans, and especially our Protestant brethren in Prussia, believe the Vatican to favour the Allies in this terrible conflict, and it would be extremely bad if I were known to have spoken with you."

"But you *are* on our side, aren't you, Your Holiness?" I immediately regretted having said this. I felt like a maggot, although His Holiness' expression did not change at all, nor did his posture.

"It might have been easier to choose sides three years ago, when the War began," said the Pope. "But both sides have rejected my attempts to bring about peace. God does not dwell where victory is the goal at all costs, not peace. I must make all attempts still to uphold the appearance of the Vatican's neutrality, and that for a very good reason."

I swallowed. My mouth was dry, like an engine that hasn't been oiled in a while. "What reason is that, Your Holiness?"

"Because it is true." Pope Benedict turned to Hat. "Enrico, please find a glass of water for Signore McCracken. And that book on the table in the hall, if you please." Enrico bowed and left the room. The Pope smiled. "I must overlook some of Enrico's more colourful activities in the past," he explained, spreading his hands wide. "His reputation for loyalty and secrecy is unparalleled in anyone I have ever met."

My eyes widened. "Is he Mafia?" I asked.

"He was." His Holiness shrugged. "Every saint has a past, every sinner a future. Was it not Oscar Wilde who wrote that, Signore McCracken?"

I grimaced. "He wasn't a very good man, Your Holiness."

"But when he died, he was a faithful son of the Church," observed the Pope, "and although he spoke much that was irrelevant, he also loved the truth." The Pope smiled. "That is why, in his final days, he returned to his true Mother."

I cleared my throat. "This Enrico, Your Holiness," I said, "he pulled a gun on me."

The Pope nodded with great wisdom. "That was always a risk," he said, "but I knew he would not use it."

"How could you be certain?"

"It was not loaded. The gun—how should we say this?—makes him feel comfortable, but I have forbidden him to put bullets in it."

The door opened and Enrico returned with a glass of water, which I gulped down.

Pope Benedict held up the book Enrico had handed him and showed me the cover. The title was in German, and a red ribbon marked a place in it. "Are you familiar with the works of Karl Marx and Friedrich Engels, Signore McCracken?"

I shook my head. "I'm afraid not, Your Holiness, though I have heard their names."

The Pope turned the book over and meditated upon the cover for a moment. "The title of this one in English is *The Communist Manifesto*. Let me read you a short passage. And please excuse me, but I must translate from German into English for you. I will be slow." He opened the book, moved the ribbon aside, and held it so that the light caught the page. "'The Pope, the Tsar, the French radicals and the German people are all united against communism.'" He flipped the page a few times and read again: "'Communism abolishes eternal truths, it abolishes all religion and all morality.'" He turned the page again. "'Communism is the stage of historical development that makes all existing religions unnecessary and brings about their destruction.'" He closed the book and set it on the table. "Communists regard their Mother Church as their enemy, their implacable and historic foe. It matters not that she loves them, each and every one, individually and compassionately, that she loves them so much that she will endure the scorn and slander that they pour upon her. But she also loves them so much that she will not lie to them and tell them that they are correct in their beliefs. There is therefore a permanent state of war between communism and the Church."

His Holiness paused a moment, removed his glasses, rubbed his eyes, and then continued. "For three years, Signore McCracken, I have striven to bring an end to this terrible conflict, the suicide of civilized Europe. These wealthiest of all nations of God's earth are using the most dreadful weapons military science has ever devised to destroy one another with ever increasing refinements of horror. There is no limit to the slaughter, and every day the earth is drenched with newly spilt blood." He lifted the book and waved it in the air. "But now I begin to fear not so much the War as what will come when the War is over. I fear the end of the War will bring in an era of communism, an era that the so-called civilized powers of Europe, who have spent themselves in this pointless conflict, will be powerless to stop, an era of oppression, mass murders and godlessness unseen since the time of Sodom and Gomorrah. Russia—Holy Russia—is on the brink of revolution, and although no one has yet stated it, that revolution will certainly be a communist revolution. This Lenin is a committed communist, and he will not permit Russia to be anything else. Signore McCracken, I greatly fear the rise of communism. We must do everything in our power to stop it."

I wished I hadn't finished my glass of water. "You want me to stop the rise of communism?" I asked.

"I fear that is the work of more than one man," replied the Pope with a sigh. "That will be the work of nothing less than divine mercy. But there is one part of the revolution that can be turned back. The Kazanskaya. Russia has always been the faithful daughter of the Blessed Virgin. And she can be again, she can again be called Holy Russia, if the Kazanskaya is found and preserved from destruction."

"Your Holiness," I said, "I was already on my way to attempt to recover the Kazanskaya."

"I know." His Holiness nodded gravely. "I know, Signore McCracken. I did not bring you here to make a request of you, but to offer you my support. You need fuel and supplies; I can provide you with both." He smiled, and doing so seemed to lift the burden from his shoulders.

Even now, several decades later, I can't reveal the location of these supplies. His Holiness gave me no chart, no place-name, just some map coordinates. Seeing the elegantly handwritten numbers of a piece of paper almost thick enough to serve as blotting paper, Sikorsky scratched his head. "We can find it," he declared.

Serpe had wanted to accompany us on our adventure, but the war effort required both him and his aeroplane, and so permission was denied. He flew beside the LS3 for an hour after we left Venice, then dipped his wings, saluted us, and peeled away. It was with regret I saw him leave. What would happen to him and us, I had no idea at all. Disconsolate, I wandered away from the wheelhouse to the dining room, where I found Ari and Archie playing with some wooden blocks I had carved in the LS3's workshop. I had carved him a variety of triangular shapes, mostly right-angled triangles with a variety of steepness in the inclined plane, so that he could construct ramps. I had made him trapezoidal blocks so he could construct arches—arches for Archie. I had spent ages on the lathe, turning perfect cylinders and capitals in correct Doric and Ionic form. Actually, what he wanted to do was let us build towers and then knock them down, giggling.

After about half an hour, the door opened and Fritz came in, enveloped in a marvelous aroma and pushing a dining cart. He cleared his throat and spoke through the speaking tube. "Dinner is served in the *Speiseraum*."

A muffled clattering noise came from above, and seconds later Grubworthy squeezed through the doorway and took a seat at our table. "Sorry if I'm late," he apologized.

"Fritz has barely finished speaking," I observed. "You seem to have recovered remarkably well from the belladonna incident."

Grubworthy belched.

We prayed Grace. "Cadwallader," said Ari, leaning back so that Fritz could ladle soup into her bowl, "is there anything you love as much as food?"

Grubworthy actually paused for a moment and stared wistfully out of the window. The shadow of the window frame moved across his face as Sikorsky corrected the LS3's course to a new heading. At last, he said, "There was a woman once."

Ari's eyebrows jumped. "Your fiancée? Your sweetheart?"

Grubworthy shook his head. "Nothing so formal as that. She was an actress. I saw her playing a Welsh princess in one of Shakespeare's plays. I think it was called *Henry the Somethingth*. She moved like an angel, and she sang like a saint in Heaven. She wore blue, and the light caught her so that she shone, as if she had a halo." He sighed deeply. "I knew she couldn't be mine, but I knew I could be no one else's." He began spooning the soup into his mouth. "I devoted myself . . . to cuisine . . . after that," he concluded, between spoonfuls. "By the way, where are we going now?"

"After we've taken on fuel," I explained, "we're heading east, to Kazan. That's a city in Russia, where the Kazanskaya used to be kept. Maybe the monks at the monastery there can give us some clue where to find it."

"That's nice." Grubworthy ladled himself some more soup. "Fritz, this soup is excellent. Oh, where is he?" But Fritz had gone to take food to Sikorsky in the wheelhouse.

We found the lonely island, not much more than a yellow rock jutting out of the azure sea, indicated by His Holiness, and took on fuel and supplies. Then we headed east.

First, we crossed Greece. Although this was a friendly power, we cabled the Hellenic Air Force to let them know that the zeppelin crossing their territory was not an enemy. Even so, a number of curious Spads buzzed by to inspect us as we lumbered over the rocky valleys and lonely monasteries of the Peloponnese. They didn't open fire, however, and soon we left Greece behind. Passing over the Gallipoli Peninsula, where one of the most terrible battles of the War had been fought two years previously, we found ourselves flying across the Black Sea. Once, we watched a large battleship crawl beneath us, its Imperial Russian Navy ensign streaming from the stern flagpole.

Shortly after this, we turned north and spotted land a few hours later: the Crimean coast. At first, the Crimean landscape was wooded slopes and turquoise lakes, but after a while it flattened out, and we flew over mile after mile of corn fields.

"Now," smiled Sikorsky, "you have seen all Ukraine and Russia—all is the same."

"I feel very tiny, crawling over such a huge place," Ari commented.

"Smaller if down there," replied Sikorsky. "Still, is good place to learn flying."

"You had a plane when you were a boy?" I asked, puzzled, knowing that the Wright Brothers had made the first powered flight only fourteen years previously.

"*Nyet*," answered Sikorsky. "My father, he would let me drive *troika*, three-horse sled. I would make horses go faster and faster, until I was thinking, 'Now I fly!' Sometimes, I would fly all the way across our estate."

"Was it a big estate?"

Sikorsky shook his head. "Just one thousand souls. But when you are small boy, that seems very big." He pointed. "My father's estate was like this one, but up in north, near Kiev."

Below us, winding roads converged on a large house, one story only, but spread over a large area and roughly shaped like a hook. People were emerging from the house, shielding their eyes with their hands as they watched us pass by.

"You see," Sikorsky pointed out sadly, "most of people are women. Mostly, the men fight, or are dead. Holy Russia pays heavy price for this War."

We flew on over this landscape for another day, into the cooler air of the north. And when the sun was beginning to hide beyond the distant horizon, Sikorsky let us down in a field a couple of miles from the city of Kazan. I clambered down the rope ladder and tethered the airship to a tree; Sikorsky cut the engines, and peace settled over the scene.

At a gate in the hedgerow stood a man dressed in the traditional *rubakha* shirt and fur hat of the Russian peasants. His beard reached halfway down his chest. I gave him a friendly wave but his expression did not alter. I finished securing the LS3, and when I turned round again, he was gone. I climbed back up into the gondola.

Ari pushed something into my hand. "Vasili says we'll need our passports—you can't travel anywhere in Russia without one."

We decided to leave Fritz in the LS3 with Archie, while Ari, Grubworthy, Sikorsky and I took the Daimler into the city. We lowered the ramp and Fritz turned the motor-car's crank. The engine rumbled into life and we motored slowly down the ramp and into the field.

"What is this?" At Sikorsky's words, I looked up and saw a large crowd of peasants blocking the gate. They wielded clubs, pitchforks and other weapons, and they looked as if they meant business.

CHAPTER 10
PEASANTS AND MONKS

As the motor-car approached the peasants, we began to hear the angry buzz of their voices. Their faces were grim, their brows knit, their fists clenched. They seethed like a stormy sea, impatient to unleash themselves upon us. We slowed down, and several of the peasants stepped forward, holding out their hands and crying out sternly, "Stop! Stop!"

"They speak English," I observed.

"The word is same in English and Russian," answered Sikorsky.

"What do they want?" asked Grubworthy, his voice higher-pitched than usual.

Sikorsky shrugged and pulled on the brake. The motor-car rocked forward but moved no further. Sikorsky did not switch the engine off, but kept it running. The peasants milled round us, waving their clubs in the air, their faces dark with anger. One of them, who wore a peaked cap and carried an old rifle with a long bayonet, strode forward, pushing the peasants aside as he came. Planting his feet firmly, he thrust out his chest self-importantly and shouted angrily at us. Ari and Sikorsky quickly reached into their pockets and produced their passports; when

Grubworthy and I saw this, we took out our own passports too, handing them to Sikorsky, who passed them on to the guard. The guard scrutinized each one closely, his bushy moustache wagging left and right as he considered the contents of each one.

"English?" he said, turning to me.

"Scottish," I corrected him.

"*On anglyski*," Sikorsky reassured the guard, waving a hand in my face and leaning forward.

The guard looked at the other passports, while all around us the crowd grew more and more noisy and violent. The car rocked as two or three of the peasants pushed it.

The guard asked Sikorsky a question. Sikorsky answered, puzzled. Ari leaned over to me. "The guard is asking if Vasili is an aristocrat."

"He is, isn't he?"

Ari nodded. "His father owned an estate."

Sikorsky's answer seemed to inflame the peasants even more. "*Ubiytsa!*" snarled one of them, and pushed against the door of the car so it rocked back and forth on its suspension.

"*Ya ne ubiytsa!*" Sikorsky shouted back.

"Why are they calling you a murderer?" Ari asked Sikorsky.

"Murderer?" said Grubworthy and I in unison.

"They are crazy people." Sikorsky tapped the side of his head with a forefinger. "They blame aristocrats for all the deaths they have suffered in the War."

"But you haven't been here—you're not even Russian," I pointed out.

"Ukrainian, Russian—no difference to them." Several of them pushed the car again and again, rattling us around the interior worse than a ship in a storm. The motor wavered in its pitch, but didn't cut.

"Hey—stop that!" I yelled, rising in my seat.

Instantly, the guard's bayonet swept down to point directly at my throat. At the same time, one of the peasants swung his club and a loud *clang!* told me he had smashed it into the bonnet of the car. Instantly, the engine died. Sikorsky spat out a curse in Russian, and I lavished all the linguistic ingenuity for invective furnished by my Scottish ancestry upon the peasants, leaping out of the car and pushing the guard and his bayonet aside to throw open the bonnet.

"It looks like they've broken a couple of spark plugs," I lamented, staring down at the Daimler's engine. Rounding on the peasants, I hurled a stream of curses at them.

The peasants had fallen silent. Clubs that had been brandished in the air now hung limply from their hands, and the guard pulled off his cap, shamefaced. Several of them hung their heads, silent and confused. "Volodnia!" the guard said in dismay.

The peasant who had struck the car stepped forward, his head hung, and whipped off his fur hat. "*Volodnia, shto ny nadelali?*" The guard hastily pushed our passports back into our hands. "We did not know who you were, *Baritchi*," he said, glancing guiltily at the engine. "There . . . ah . . . there may be someone at the Great House who can repair it."

"I can fix it myself, thank you," I answered him shortly, noticing with some anger that he could have spoken English all along but had chosen not to. "The question is, how can we finish our journey?"

And that was how, after the peasants had helped us push the Daimler back to the LS3 and up the ramp again, we ended up in what appeared to be a dilapidated barouche, clattering over the uneven road between the hedgerows. Volodnia, who felt guilty about damaging the Daimler, had attempted to make amends by driving us to the monastery where the Kazanskaya had once been housed. Ari raised the canopy, but the roughness of the ride kept shaking it back down, and in the end she gave up and let the wind stream her long hair out behind her. Volodnia's whip flicked over the backs of the horses and they flew on towards the city. Every time we jolted over a rut in the road, it seemed, we were tossed up in the air like pancakes, and we thought it could be only moments before the roughness of the road shook the old carriage to pieces.

The monastery of Our Lady of Kazan stood on the north bank of the Volga River. Most of the buildings, that towered above the perimeter wall, were of a shining white, with golden domes rising above them. But the building nearest the gate was of red brick. Off to the left was a tiered bell-tower like a tall wedding cake. Before it was a wide open space where walked the citizens of Kazan. A few soldiers in olive-coloured uniforms stood in small groups here and there.

Volodnia tied up his team, and shook his head vigorously when Sikorsky tried to pay him. He promised to wait until we returned. Following Sikorsky, we passed through the outer gate, climbed a few steps and walked through wide doors flanked by triple Doric columns. We found ourselves in a spacious room whose walls were entirely covered with gold and icons. Candles burned everywhere. Black-robed monks rubbed shoulders with priests in gorgeous vestments and peasant women in headscarves, often carrying babies.

Sikorsky made the Sign of the Cross; it looked backwards to me, as in the Eastern Church they start on the right shoulder and cross to their left. He led us through the room and past a wide staircase to a priest whom he addressed as *Batiushka*, inclining his head in a respectful bow. The two conversed in Russian for a few moments, Ari paying close attention the whole time. At last, the priest beckoned us and conducted us out of the large room and up the stairs to a pair of large oaken doors. He knocked and, hearing a voice from within, pushed on the handle and ushered us in.

"This is study belonging to abbot," whispered Sikorsky.

The abbot was robed in black, and wore on his head a tall *kamilavka* with a veil that covered the back of his neck. His beard was perfectly white, and behind him and his desk the whole wall was covered with bookshelves. Some of the books were ancient, their titles written by hand in Cyrillic. A large grey cat slumbered on a fur rug before a cold fireplace. Having seen that we were hardly worth noticing, the cat returned to sleep.

Sikorsky bowed deeply to the abbot, who had risen and circled his desk to greet us. We followed suit, and the abbot said a blessing in Russian over each of us. Then he bowed to us as deeply as Sikorsky had bowed. Grubworthy looked a little uneasy at receiving his blessing and managed only an awkward half-bow.

"Welcome, my sons, my daughter," said the abbot in English. "You have traveled very far and you must be weary. May I offer you some refreshment? We have some *kvass.*"

"That would be lovely, thank you," said Ari.

The abbot poured us all some of the dark liquid and handed the glasses round, inviting us to sit around the fireplace. The kvass was tangy and sour, in a kind of pickled cucumber sort of way, and a complete surprise, but delicious once you got used to it.

"*Batiushka*," began Sikorsky, "we need your help." He quickly explained why we were in Russia.

"Ah!" The abbot sighed deeply. "If the Kazanskaya could be found, what joy! What is Holy Russia without the Blessed Virgin to follow? But are you sure of this, my friends? This quest is not to be undertaken lightly. It will require the utmost reverence on your part."

"I think we can find it, if it can be found," I assured him.

The abbot smiled. "Many people have sought God, but found that what they seek is not really Him. It might be wealth, or success, or the good opinion of friends or colleagues. But sooner or later, the very holiest of people find God by allowing Him to find them."

"Are you suggesting that we find the icon by not looking for it?" I turned, surprised, for it had been Grubworthy who had spoken.

"Not at all," returned the abbot. "But even if you are in the right place, you will not necessarily find the Kazanskaya. She will find you, and you must wait respectfully for her."

"Do you have any clue what might have happened to the Kazanskaya?" I asked.

The abbot's brow wrinkled. "I know very little, alas. But there is someone here who may be able to help you: Elder Zosimus. He may remember the man who stole the Virgin."

"Can you take us to him?"

"Of course." The abbot rose from his seat. "Come." He led us out of the study, down some steps and through a narrow door into the open air. We found ourselves in a wide courtyard. To our right was a three-story building, whitewashed, that appeared to be living quarters for the monks; to our left rose the magnificent marble of the church, all ionic columns and golden domes. The faithful were just leaving after the liturgy, the women removing their veils as they emerged. They were a mixed bunch, mainly peasants, but with a few well-dressed ladies and gentlemen among them, who watched us curiously as we crossed the courtyard with the abbot.

"Are you well, Grubworthy?" I asked.

"Perfectly well, thank you, McCracken," he replied. But falling into step with me, he lowered his voice and said, "But all this—this worshiping of art and so forth. Doesn't it seem a little superstitious to you? I mean, I know you're a Papist and all that, but this seems so much worse."

"Worse?"

"Perhaps that's the wrong word. But certainly more superstitious. All those pictures, all those candles."

"Grubworthy, what faith are you?"

"Me? I'm Church of England. At least, I was. I haven't been to a service in years."

I took a deep breath. "An icon," I explained, trying to remember what Sikorsky had explained to us, "is a bit like a sacrament. You have sacraments in the Church of England, don't you?"

"Of course," responded Grubworthy quickly. But a puzzled expression descended between his eyebrows. "Baptism and holy communion."

"Well, there are more than that—marriage, holy orders, last rites, confession, confirmation." Grubworthy continued to look puzzled. In fact, his puzzlement seemed to increase. "It's an outward sign of an inward grace." I dug down deep to find the words that would mean something to him. "Through a sacrament, you make actual contact with God Himself. Through an icon, someone of the Orthodox faith believes he can actually see the eternal. It's much more than just a picture."

Grubworthy nodded. "That's what I mean. It all sounds so superstitious. How can you see God? He's a spirit, isn't He?"

By this time, we had walked around the third large building off the courtyard to the perimeter wall, where the abbot unlatched a gate. We followed him through it and onto a wooded path. Grubworthy fell behind me and our conversation ceased for the time being. Off to our right, we could hear the

Volga rushing by, and sometimes we glimpsed it through the leafy branches. In time, we came upon a little stone hut with a thatched roof, two windows, and a low door between them. Beneath the windows, a crowd of red and white roses nodded their heads in the breeze.

Before we had even reached the threshold, the door opened and an old man emerged. His eyes were like a pair of bright stars, from which wrinkles fanned outwards through his nut-brown face. He was mostly bald, but a fringe of white hair stuck out over his ears as if afraid to lie flat. His beard was sparse but hung almost to his waist. He was short, and leaned on a knobbled but shiny walking stick.

"I knew you would come," the Elder Zosimus greeted us. "I knew you would come to recover the Virgin of Kazan! I saw you, sailing in your ship of silver through the air, like the Fool of the World, across all Russia!"

"You saw us?" I asked, incredulous.

The elder nodded wisely. "*She* showed me. The Lady told me you would come. She showed me the ship that sails on clouds. I knew you would come seeking the Virgin of Kazan."

While I still stood amazed, the abbot said goodbye, and Elder Zosimus invited us into the hut. I leaned close to Sikorsky. "What exactly is an elder?" I asked in a whisper. "A prophet or something like that?"

"Is kind of hermit," replied the Ukrainian, "very wise. They live alone, though they are often attached to monasteries. People come to elders all the time for blessings and for advice. But there are not many left now, not many at all."

We found ourselves in a smallish room with another door opposite the one we had come through, which presumably led to the elder's bedroom. The furniture was crude, and nothing more than was absolutely necessary. There were old mahogany chairs with worn leather upholstery, upon which the elder bade us sit, while he reclined upon an old-fashioned settee. Two flower pots stood on one of the window-sills, and in them grew marigolds. In one corner stood a small table, upon which was set a samovar and stacks of plates and cups. Near it was a stove, such as you might see in any Russian house, with an oven at waist height and a hatch for wood directly below it. Wood was stacked neatly at its side, and a kettle stood on the top surface. In another corner of the room hung a very large icon of Mary, before which burned an icon lamp. It was surrounded by a host of smaller icons and a few statues of saints and angels. Over the door of the bedroom was a crucifix with the inscription and the foot-rest you see on Orthodox crucifixes.

"Now," said Elder Zosimus, "speak, children."

Sikorsky and I explained why we were here, and Elder Zosimus did not interrupt us at all until we described our confrontation with the mob of peasants. At this, he clicked his tongue and shook his head sadly. "The Russian peasant is very dutiful, very loyal, very honest. But for fifty years, ever since the Emancipation, they have done this—formed mobs and rebelled. Rebelled against their masters, against their fathers, against their Church and their God. I think they do not properly understand what it means to be free—and into this misunderstanding, Satan inserts his evil spirit, the spirit of rebellion."

"Evil spirit?"

"An evil spirit," repeated Elder Zosimus. "I say it again: an evil spirit, sent by Satan to turn the people of Russia away from the Church, away from the Truth, away from God. They did not want to harm you or your motor-car. They were compelled to do it, compelled, I say, by an evil spirit of rebellion." He sat back on his settee. "But this is not why you have flown like a cloud to this place."

"Father," said Sikorsky, "the abbot tells us you know something of the theft of the Virgin of Kazan."

"Ask. If I may answer, I shall."

"Who stole the blessed icon?"

"The man who stole it is called Arkady Chaikin. He was not from Kazan, but from Siberia. But he moved away from Siberia and became a bank clerk here in Kazan." Elder Zosimus smiled sadly. "A good man, but very poor, for they do not pay bank clerks well. He lived in a hovel with his family. He could barely afford food for his children. But his wife, who was from Kazan herself, visited this monastery frequently to pray, and told him of the beauty of the Virgin of Kazan. Long did his mind work upon her description of the gold and jewels in the frame."

"His wife told him?" I was curious. "Didn't he see it himself?"

"Chaikin was not a man of God. He was from a part of Siberia where there are many different faiths—not just the Orthodox faith, but Islam too, and Buddhism. Perhaps by now his beliefs have changed." The elder took a deep breath and looked up towards the ceiling for a moment. "No, I am certain. I know he has faith now. I know he believes."

"How do you know?" inquired Grubworthy.

"I know. I *know*."

"What did he confess?" asked Grubworthy.

The elder did not reply, but looked calmly at Grubworthy for a long while in silence. In the end, Elder Zosimus said, "If you wish to know where Chaikin discarded the Virgin, you must ask him. It might still be there."

"Do you know where it is?" Grubworthy had spoken again and I began to wish I'd instructed him to be silent.

Elder Zosimus nodded. "Of course, I cannot tell you, because of the circumstances in which I heard. That is why the Virgin has remained where she is for more than ten years. I cannot leave this place, nor can I tell anyone where she is."

"But that's ridicu—"

"Grubworthy, enough!" I growled.

"After he had confessed to me, Chaikin turned himself in to the police. The Chief of Police may have a record of his whereabouts. If not—and records are not always well kept in Kazan—you may have to travel to St. Petersburg, where Chaikin stood trial. But the location of the Kazanskaya is not mine to reveal."

"Thank you, *Batiushka*," said Sikorsky. "You have been very helpful."

The elder nodded. "By the grace of God," he concluded. He looked at us all once more with those bright eyes and for longest at Grubworthy. "I know the Father Abbot has told you this already, but if you seek the Virgin, you must take care. There will be trouble soon—for Russia and for the world. I feel it. Our Great Mother stirs. She wishes to prevent this evil from descending upon us all. But are there enough men of good will in the world left to heed her? This spirit of rebellion, it must be rejected. Now is the time of strict obedience, for the very deepest and truest faith. Finding where the icon is can only be part of the solution. The rest must come from within."

Once we were outside, Grubworthy said, "It's preposterous that he can't just tell us where the icon is, with the fate of his nation in the balance. And all because of some silly rules!"

"A priest can't reveal what he's heard in confession," explained Ari, "not for any reason at all, under any circumstances. We'll all just have to deal with the consequences."

"Well, I call it downright silly," muttered Grub-worthy. Ari's eyes flashed but she restrained herself and no one else spoke for the rest of our walk back to the Father Abbot's study.

Father Abbot invited us to supper and offered us rooms for the night, which we accepted with joy. First, though, we had to visit the Chief of Police to read Chaikin's record, if possible, and then we had to collect Fritz and Archie. Instructing Volodnia to take us to the police station, we found ourselves once more clattering over cobblestoned streets.

Another carriage was drawn up in front of the police station, and I reached forward to put my hand on Volodnia's shoulder. He brought the barouche to a halt some distance from the police station.

"What is it, McCracken?" asked Sikorsky.

"I don't know," I answered. "Something doesn't seem quite right."

We all peered forward. The sun was getting low and there were shadows under the buildings. One of the horses yoked to the carriage outside the police station snorted and stamped one of its fore-hoofs.

People still hurried back and forth, but they looked tired, as if they just wanted to get home.

The door of the police station opened, and I instinctively ducked. The man that emerged wore a greatcoat and his head was bandaged, but he was undoubtedly Von Krems, and with him was Rabotnik.

CHAPTER 11
THE WRECKERS

Von Krems and Rabotnik climbed up into their carriage, which bobbed a little on its suspension as the large Russian took his seat. Von Krems tossed a package of papers onto the seat beside him and leaned forward to speak with the driver.

"I'll bet anything that's Chaikin's police report."

Ari looked at me sidelong. "How can you be so calm?" she asked.

I shrugged. "What's done is done," I answered. "If we don't find the information we need here, we'll just go to St. Petersburg, that's all."

Von Krems' driver flicked his whip over the horses' backs. The carriage rattled off down the street and turned right.

"Sikorsky," I said, "can you have Volodnia follow Von Krems?" Sikorsky frowned. "It's a hunch," I explained. "I can't explain it. We can go to the police station later."

Sikorsky gave some instructions to Volodnia in Russian, and in a moment we had headed off after Von Krems' carriage.

The street onto which Von Krems had turned was narrower than the one we left, the buildings three and four stories high. They looked like south-ern European buildings from the last century, in Monaco or places like that, except that they had been painted wild colours, like tangerine and teal. The sun was low, and violet shadows lay across the street, except that whenever Von Krems' carriage drove through a junction, golden light flashed over it. Sometimes, down these side-streets, we would glimpse the dome of a church or mosque. Pedestri-ans were few now, and we never saw a motor-car—the Daimler would have stood out.

Sikorsky frowned as the carriage we followed took a right turn. "This place I know. Is near mon-astery."

At that moment, a shrill mechanical sound pierced the air. "That was a steam whistle," I told the others, who had looked quizzically at me.

We turned again, and found ourselves facing the monastery. In the short time we had been away, a large crowd had gathered in front of its gates, and over their heads I could see the spindly arm of a crane or steam-shovel. The crowd murmured, a su-surration of anxiety and curiosity.

The carriage bearing Von Krems slowed but did not stop. The crowd parted for it, like the sea around the prow of a ship, then closed in behind it. Sikorsky tapped Volodnia on the shoulder and he drew rein. We stopped next to a streetcar, which seemed to have been abandoned while its driver and passengers joined the crowd. We all got down from the barouche.

"What's going on?" A crease had appeared between Ari's brows.

"Let's find out." We were about ten yards from the back of the crowd, which grew all the time. I plunged into it, followed by the others. I noticed one woman in a head-scarf, holding an infant about the same age as Archie, who was crying, while her husband attempted to comfort her. The further we went, the more densely-packed were the people, and our progress slowed to almost nothing. I turned to speak with Sikorsky, but we had been separated. Reaching backwards, I took Ari's hand so we wouldn't be split up.

Suddenly, we could go no further. The crowd stopped abruptly about twenty yards short of the monastery gate. Facing the crowd stood a line of soldiers, dressed in olive uniforms, with fur hats. Their rifles were lowered at the crowd, long bayonets gleaming evilly. Off to our right, the Father Abbot and brothers stood together in a group. Some of them wailed and tore their hair, others covered their faces.

"What is happening?" Sikorsky and Grubworthy had joined us at the front of the crowd. I was about to answer when the steam whistle blew again and I looked round sharply. It was not a crane, nor a steam-shovel, but a mobile wrecking ball mounted on a truck's chassis and powered by a steam engine. I caught my breath in horror.

Von Krems was speaking with an officer, dressed in a long greatcoat. His fur hat had a tall point on the top and a red star on the front, and three red flashes blazed on the front of his coat. A sabre hung at his side and he held a megaphone in his right hand.

"Those are not imperial troops," Sikorsky said.

"Then what are they?" I asked.

"Bolsheviks," said Ari. "Communists. The revolution has begun."

"Is possible." Sikorsky watched the unfolding drama for a few moments, while the crowd murmured all around us.

The officer saluted Von Krems and climbed up onto the cab of the wrecking ball. Lifting the megaphone to his lips, he spoke swiftly to the crowd. Sikorsky translated for us: "'You will see there is no God.' He says this, not I." Sikorsky was visibly agitated, and his voice shook as he continued his translation: "We will destroy the church of the so-called protectress of Russia and nothing will happen."

With that, the wrecking ball cranked back and swung into the double gate of the monastery. With a crash, the iron buckled inwards. A sigh rippled through the crowd, a gasp of horror. Several people close by, including Sikorsky, made the Sign of the Cross. Most of the brothers were on their knees now, beating their chests or clasping their hands in prayer. The ball swung again, and this time the masonry above the gateway crumbled and fell to the ground in a terrible cloud of white. The gates wavered and then crashed to the ground.

"I can't watch this," said Ari. "Mac, what can we do?"

"Sikorsky, are you armed?" Sikorsky shook his head. A tear had beaded in the corner of his eye. "Neither am I. Grubworthy? Never mind."

"I am." Ari was pale with anger and revulsion. "I have TNT, tear gas, and my derringer."

The ball struck again, and the wall groaned. The officer spoke.

"He asks, 'Where is your God now?'" explained Sikorsky. "He tells them that they must trust their government to look after them, not a being from mythology." The ball swung again and with a hideous rumble a whole section of wall collapsed. We could see the monastery buildings through the gap, as if through the smoke of battle.

"The Pope was right," I said bleakly. "This is terrible."

"But what can we do?" Ari's voice rose over the rending crash of yet another impact. The driver of the wrecking ball backed up a little to work on a new section of wall.

"McCracken?"

I turned towards the sound of my own name, and found myself staring into Von Krems' face. The look on his face was not surprise, but delight and victory mixed. He raised an arm and pointed. Rabotnik followed his gaze, saw me, and reached into his pocket. For a moment that seemed to stretch into hours, I could not move. But Rabotnik had barely taken his hand, his fingers wrapped about the dark sphere of a cannonball, out of his pocket, when I shouted, "Let's go!" and ducked back into the crowd.

"But Mac . . . " began Ari. I grabbed her wrist and dragged her after me. Seeing what was going on, Sikorsky followed quickly, pulling on Grubworthy. Of course, Grubworthy didn't move. Then he saw Rabotnik, cried out, turned, and ploughed into the crowd. People flew out of his path like ninepins from a bowling ball.

For me, though, fighting through the crowd was like swimming through porridge. For every person who stepped aside for us, another two would push back or not even notice we were trying to get through. Some of them wept to see the monastery demolished. Others had dropped to their knees. One woman held what looked like a Rosary, and was praying fervently, invoking the Name of Jesus over and over again. A few, mostly young men who looked like university students, chatted and laughed.

"McCracken!" Von Krems' voice boomed out from behind us. "Halt!"

"Not likely," I muttered, dodging left and right to avoid folks in the crowd. Ari, who had realized what was happening by now, followed without having to be dragged, but I had lost sight of Grubworthy and Sikorsky.

At that moment a volley of gunshots crashed out. Some in the crowd screamed, and most flattened themselves against the ground. The cordon of soldiers had fired over their heads, and now they lowered the barrels of their rifles and virtually in unison cocked them again.

I suddenly realized that the four of us, the only ones left standing, were now easy targets. The next shots would be aimed at us, and there was nothing to block the soldiers' view.

It was then I noticed Ari was missing. Spinning round, I called out her name. With a rising sense of panic, I scanned the prostrate human forms around us.

The rifles of the soldiers began to rise.

There was Ari, bent over the ground. Had she been shot? I bounded towards her, my heart racing. Two dozen dark muzzles bore down on us. Von Krems had climbed up the side of the wrecking ball, his eyes glaring.

Ari had slid aside the secret compartment in the heel of her boot and removed something. Now she jumped to her feet, drew her arm back and threw whatever it was with all her strength. As it spun through the air, it flashed in the aging rays of the sun. Then Ari turned and sped away, leaping over the people on the ground like a hurdler.

"Come on, Mac, what are you waiting for?" she shouted over her shoulder.

Something exploded right in front of the wrecking ball, and a grey cloud billowed up and out from it. Von Krems cried out in alarm and tumbled over backwards from the wrecking ball, his arms flying out to his sides. Yells of alarm and pain erupted from everybody nearby.

"God bless tear gas," I said and dashed after Ari.

But not everyone had been engulfed by Ari's secret weapon, and rifle shots cracked out in an uncoordinated way from either side behind us. Bullets whizzed past my ears and one ploughed into the cobbled pavement right in front of my feet, sending up a little plume of dust and stone. I began to weave.

Reaching the street by which we had arrived, I stooped low, hit the ground, and rolled. Springing to a kneeling position, I scanned the street for Volodnia.

Volodnia was gone, and the barouche with him.

The streetcar we had seen earlier still stood there, next to the empty space where the barouche had been. The horses of the streetcar pranced and tossed their heads, alarmed by the gunshots. The whites of their eyes glowed in the purple shadows cast by the buildings. Ari and I dived for cover behind the streetcar, just as a hail of bullets rattled around it. One of the windows shattered.

"Where's Volodnia?" Ari panted.

"Where indeed?" I returned.

Sikorsky and Grubworthy now joined us. "Can't we leave?" wailed Grubworthy. "They're shooting at us."

"Yes, I noticed that." I ran my eyes over the street behind us for an escape route. "Perhaps you could ask them to stop. I can't imagine where Volodnia's gone."

Something inside me, some sixth sense, urged me to duck, and the moment I did, a heavy object struck the streetcar like a meteor where my head had been. Splinters of wood showered over my head and shoulders. All four of us cried out in alarm, for a cannonball had embedded itself in the wall of the streetcar.

"Rabotnik is behind us!" I said.

"Is anywhere safe?" asked Grubworthy.

I pointed. "There, perhaps." We dashed off to the right, where a deserted side-street, branching off from this thoroughfare, ran parallel to the monastery wall.

But we had not got far when soldiers appeared at the far end of the street. Seeing us, they stopped and raised their rifles. A couple of shots rang out; a bullet sent up a little cloud of dust near my feet.

"This way!" Sikorsky headed for a fence made of planks of wood, about six feet high. He found an iron handle and pulled, leading us into a narrow alleyway between two houses. Our footsteps echoed, the rasping of our breath was magnified—it seemed that all of Russia must surely hear us! In a few moments, we had reached the far end. Sikorsky threw open the gate and we emerged into the long shadows of another street, very much like the last one we'd been on. It was slightly wider, and a few businesses were interspersed with private houses. Yellow lights glowed from some windows.

"They'll be here in a moment." Ari cocked an ear. Behind the fence, in the alleyway, we could hear the tramp of boots.

Sikorsky reached out and tried a door handle. The door refused to budge. We dashed on to the next door. It too was locked. We ran on. In a square of light, we saw a woman's face. Sikorsky knocked on the door instead of rattling the handle.

Behind us, the gate of the alleyway began to move.

The house door opened, and the woman we had seen through the window stood there. Her eyes were red, as if she had been weeping. Sikorsky spoke to her rapidly and quietly in Russian, glancing towards the alleyway. She followed his gaze. The gate had been flung wide open. She stepped aside, and we piled into her house. The door gave a soft bang as it closed.

The room we stood in was a little like the hermitage: plain wooden floor, plain wooden walls, with an icon in the corner and a stove on which a pot bubbled aromatically. A red and white checkered tablecloth was spread over a table, which was set for supper, and a cuckoo clock hung on the wall. It was a corner house, so it had windows on two sides. I crossed to one window and peered out at an empty street, while Ari stood guard at the front window. The lady of the house stood looking at us, wringing her hands.

Outside, men's voices shouted harshly to each other as the soldiers emerged from the alleyway and began searching for us.

I made the Sign of the Cross and prayed for a miracle.

CHAPTER 12
CHASED BY COSSACKS

Ari peeked through the window. "They're trying each of the doors in turn," she said. "They'll try this one any second.

"Lock the door!" whined Grubworthy.

Ari turned a wrinkled brow towards him. "And then what? What do you think they'll say? 'This one's locked, move on to the next?'" She shook her head. "They'll just break the door in, and then this lady will have no door when the winter comes."

"But it will slow them down, at least."

"Quiet!" I hissed, and pointed through the window by which I stood. "How did he get here?" Everyone crowded around me and peered through the window. In the other street, the one the soldiers were not searching yet, stood a monk. He was walking slowly towards us, blinking and looking left and right as if searching for something but he didn't know what. "Maybe he can help us."

Carefully, so as to make as little noise as possible, we pushed open the door to the side street. "*Spasiba*," said Sikorsky to the woman behind us. Then we closed the door and crossed the street towards the monk.

The monk stared at us for a moment, his eyes wide. He was evidently terrified. His eyes refocused on us and he said with a stammer, "M-McCracken?"

"That's me," I replied. Then I added, "*Da.*"

The monk started talking fast in Russian, his eyes darting back and forth as he spoke. Sikorsky answered. The monk pointed back the way he had come. A light seemed to switch on behind Sikorsky's eyes as he turned to the rest of us.

"There is escape route," he explained. "Brother Andrei was sent to find us."

"Escape route? Where?"

"This way." Brother Andrei and Sikorsky led us along the street towards a tavern. It was low-roofed and timbered inside, with many icons and pictures of country life on the walls. Two windows looked out on the street and opposite them was the bar. Behind the bar were shelves on which stood bottles of various sizes and colours. A balalaika and an accordion rested in one corner. At one of the tables sat a man with a grey beard, who nursed a large glass of vodka. Like the woman who had hidden us, he seemed emotionally devastated, his eyes rimmed with red, the vodka in the glass trembling as if it were on a railway line. Seeing us, he rose from his seat.

"Mackrensky?" he asked.

"McCracken," I replied, nodding.

The tavern-owner led us behind the bar, talking all the time, while Sikorsky nodded and nodded in reply. The tavern-owner pulled on a trapdoor, lit a lantern, and led us into his cellar.

"See how Our Lady has favoured us!" observed Sikorsky. "There is tunnel from this tavern to monastery grounds. It was dug during reign of Ivan the Terrible."

The tavern-owner stooped as if he were going to draw from one of the large barrels, but then he pulled on the tap. The front of the cask was hinged and opened outwards like a door. He stood aside and, thanking him, we all filed past him and into the dark. As I passed, he touched my arm and I looked into his face. He spoke to me earnestly in Russian, and I looked to Sikorsky for a translation.

"He says, if you can find Our Lady of Kazan, you must do it, and prevent these barbarians from taking over Holy Russia. Only she can do it. He says, Thank you."

I put what I hoped was a reassuring hand on the tavern-keeper's shoulder. "I'll do my best, by God's grace." Sikorsky translated. The tavern-keeper nodded and handed the lantern to Brother Andrei, who took the lead.

It was indeed a very old tunnel, we found as we crept along it. Timbers, damp and rotten in places, shored up the ceiling, and the lantern picked out graffiti in Russian that looked centuries old. The ground was muddy, the air clammy. Even in the summer, it was cold.

"Why was that woman crying?" asked Grubworthy in a tremulous voice out of the dimness.

"She weeps to see monastery destroyed," answered Sikorsky. "The tavern-keeper also. They grieve because it seems Holy Russia dies."

Ari and I made the Sign of the Cross.

A few moments later, we climbed a few uneven steps, the monk rattled a door handle, and a square of blue light appeared before us. We emerged into the monastery grounds not far from the hermitage. The monk said something to us and quickly shut the door again, leaving us in the long shadows of the trees, the Volga rushing along not far away.

The door to the hermitage opened, and Elder Zosimus stood in the frame, beckoning. "Come quickly!" he urged us. "Come!"

A dog barked behind us, and we heard bodies moving through the undergrowth. Soldiers were approaching through the trees from the direction of the monastery buildings. We sped across the little lawn and into the hermitage.

Elder Zosimus closed the door and ushered us through his front room and into the bedroom at the back of the house. Another door opened onto a neat little garden with beans growing on one side and half a dozen beehives standing on the other. At the far end of the narrow path was a wall with a gate in it. Elder Zosimus opened the gate.

"Go with God," he said. "Russia groans, but perhaps you can save the icon. You can save the Holy Mother! Be blessed in your travels." And he gave each of us a blessing as we passed through the gate and out of the monastery.

Under the wall waited the grinning Volodnia, seated upon his dilapidated barouche.

"He didn't abandon us!" I exclaimed in delight and surprise.

"Of course not," answered Sikorsky. "He is loyal Russian peasant."

We all climbed into the barouche. I tried to raise the hood, but there was nothing to latch it onto, and I had to leave it folded. Volodnia called something to the horses, and a moment later we were speeding off along the street, away from the monastery and away from Von Krems and Rabotnik and the Bolshevik soldiers.

At least, so we thought. For as we turned a corner that should have led us away from town, we found ourselves confronted by a cordon of soldiers, all mounted, rifles hanging from their saddles and sabres drawn.

Seeing us, one of them gave a cry and with a flick of the heels they came galloping towards us.

Volodnia saw them and responded instantly. He pulled on the reins so that the horses' heads turned to the left. For a moment, we still hurtled towards them; then the barouche began to swing around in as tight a U-turn as I'd ever seen accomplished by horses.

At the extremity of the turn, the barouche lurched. It seemed as if every seam in the coachwork, every screw and nail and rivet, jumped a little. The whole vehicle clattered, wood and steel and leather. The carriage brushed the hedgerow, sticks and leaves flying in a cloud about us.

As we straightened out from the turn and started galloping away from the soldiers, I felt a shudder beneath me and leaned out over the side of the barouche. One of the wheels wobbled unsteadily.

"Sikorsky!" I shouted. "Tell Volodnia that the right rear wheel is working loose!"

Sikorsky exchanged a few words with our driver, then shouted over his shoulder: "He say, Hit wheel hub with hammer."

"What hammer?" The barouche jolted over a bump in the road and a wooden box slid out from under my seat. In it were a pair of pliers, a vice-clamp, and a few other dirty tools, including a mallet. "Oh, that one." I took it and leaned over the side of the barouche.

"Mac!" At the sound of Ari's voice, I turned quickly. One of the soldiers had caught up with us. His eyes glinted like his sabre as he raised it over Ari's head.

Without thinking, I flung the mallet at him. It hit him square in the forehead, and with a yell of pain he toppled backwards over the crupper of his saddle and disappeared from view. His horse galloped on beside us for a few paces, then slowed and was left behind.

"Well done," said Ari. "Now how will you fix the wheel?"

"How about, 'Well done, Mac, what a good shot?'" I asked.

"McCracken, behind you!" wailed Grubworthy.

I spun about, to find that yet another soldier had caught up with us. His eyes were wild, his nostrils flared as he reached out and caught hold of the door of the barouche. He pulled himself out of his saddle and towards us, clamping his sabre between his teeth.

The hinges of the door sprang apart. The soldier yelled, his sabre flying away into the darkness. He tumbled into the road. Behind us, one of our remaining pursuers leaped over his prostrate comrade and continued the chase.

"Ari, do you still have some TNT left?" The horsemen were gaining visibly on us. The one in the lead was a particularly good rider—he and the horse seemed to move as a single mechanism.

Ari reached down and slid aside the heel of her boot. The TNT charge was very small, about two inches long. But I knew it was enough to do some real damage if I could just time it right and throw it accurately. "Does anyone have a match?" asked Ari.

We all searched our pockets, but none of us were smokers.

The lead soldier pulled up alongside us. I saw his knee rise and his foot press against his saddle as he raised himself to a standing position on the horse's back. He clutched his sabre in one hand and held the other out for balance.

"Great Scott!" I lamented.

Volodnia cast a glance at him over his shoulder. "*Proklyatiy Kazak*," he muttered.

Sikorsky said, "He say—"

"I know what he said, Vasili," interrupted Ari.

The Cossack sprang from the saddle, through the broken door and into the barouche. Its whole frame rattled at the impact and something fell off the undercarriage—I've no idea what. The Cossack slashed at me with his sabre. I saw a silver blur inches from my eyes as I dodged backwards, and heard the blade hiss through the air. He held the sword out fully extended, its point almost touching my throat. The barouche jolted over bumps in the road, and we all lurched and swayed with it except him— the Cossack remained perfectly steady. I saw his muscles tense as he prepared to thrust home.

A deafening *bang!* shattered our eardrums and with a metallic ding the sword spun out of the Cossack's grasp. The wind caught the tiny curl of smoke at the muzzle of Ari's derringer and flung it behind the barouche. The Cossack reeled backwards, clutching his hand, which the bullet's impact with his sword had stung. I stepped forward and aimed a blow at his chin. He took a step back, but when I tried to follow up on my attack he was ready and stayed out of my range. I over-extended. He side-swiped me. I toppled backwards into a seat. The Cossack reached for my throat, but I raised a foot and pushed him away. "Ouch!" cried Grubworthy as the Cossack landed in his lap.

At this point, the other rider, who had been gaining on us, drew up beside the barouche. He sprang. With a rattle and a thump, he alighted in the carriage. One of the floorboards broke under him, but he regained his balance in a moment.

Sikorsky said something vicious in Russian and leaped out of the seat beside Volodnia to attack the newcomer. But I didn't have time to see what happened next.

The Cossack and I had lurched to our feet at the same time. We closed and grappled each other for a few moments, our feet slipping on the barouche's floor.

Something bumped hard into my back, and I turned sharply about. It was Sikorsky, who had also spun around upon our collision. Sikorsky threw a punch at the Cossack and I laid into the other.

"Will you people keep still!" yelled Ari, her derringer wavering between one Russian and the other.

The barouche left the ground a moment as it met a bump in the road. We all ducked to maintain our balance. The old leather canopy in the back of the barouche opened like a fan for a moment and then clattered shut as we hit the road again. We all sprawled in the bottom of the carriage. When I climbed to my feet, I was facing the Cossack again. He grabbed me by the front of my shirt and swung me to the floor so that my shoulders were in the opening where the door had been.

The Cossack was strong; I could feel him pressing me down. Wind flew past my face, whipping my hair about, and I could see the road flashing by inches from my head. The Cossack grinned and pushed down with his thick hands. I choked. I couldn't get any air at all.

Suddenly, the Cossack screamed and released me. For a moment, I did not realize what had happened. Then I saw what amazed me, that Grubworthy had taken the pliers out of the toolbox and with the deftness with which I had seen him nabbing mushrooms in the officers' club in Venice, neatly pinched and twisted the Cossack's ear with them. The Cossack got to his feet, blood running between the fingers with which he clutched his ear. He turned on Grubworthy. With a back-handed swipe, he smacked the portly Englishman across the face.

Howling, Grubworthy staggered backwards and toppled out of the barouche. As he fell, he managed to grap one of the leather folds of the canopy. It immediately enveloped him like a hammock and dangled him over the back of the barouche.

All that weight in the rear of the barouche was more than the poor vehicle could take. The loose wheel finally flew off its axle and bounced away back along the road. The underside of the barouche dropped sharply, hit the road with a grinding bang and bounced. The Cossack staggered back onto Ari, who shoved him aside onto me. I drove my knee up into his belly and he crumpled in half. With a push, I tossed him out of the barouche.

In the meantime, Sikorsky and the other soldier fell in an awkward mass of limbs to the floor of the carriage. Grubworthy's arms groped towards the barouche as he fought to regain his position inside it. Meanwhile, Sikorsky was on his feet faster than the soldier. He picked him up by the back of the jacket and thrust him through the open doorway into the road. Ari and I together hauled on Grubworthy and rolled him onto the floor of the barouche.

"Well, that wasn't what I expected," remarked Grubworthy. "What jolly fun!"

Volodnia flicked his whip over the horses' backs and they continued their headlong flight. The corner of the barouche, scraping along the road, sent up a thick cloud of dust and wood-chips behind us.

Volodnia pulled on the reins. We turned and found ourselves in the field where we had landed earlier that day. Before us rose the impressive bulk of the LS3, Fritz framed in light from the doorway. Archie held his hand.

"*Spasiba*, Volodnia," I said to our driver. "I'm sorry about the damage to your barouche."

Sikorsky translated and Volodnia replied with a few words and a wide, gap-toothed grin. "He say, he damage your motor-car, you damage his barouche. Now you are even."

Volodnia kissed each one of us on either cheek and we climbed the rope ladder into the gondola of the LS3. Behind us, we could hear the engines of several trucks. Sikorsky dashed into the wheelhouse.

"Fritz, cast off!" I shouted. Fritz passed Archie to Ari and hastened to cast off our moorings while I climbed up onto the gantry that led to the Mercedes engines. The ground was dropping away below us as three trucks trundled into the field and Bolshevik soldiers spilled out.

I reached up for the blade of the propeller and thrust it downwards. The engine sputtered a little, but did not catch. I tried again, ducking away from the blades. This time the engine roared and the propeller spun. I raced across the stern of the gondola to the next engine.

Below us, the soldiers raised their rifles and a smattering of gunshots crackled in the night. The muzzle flashes were almost pretty, I thought, as I summoned the second engine to life. But I knew we were relatively safe. Ordinary bullets couldn't hope to penetrate the skin of the LS3.

Even as I thought that, a bullet hissed by my ear and ricocheted from the wall of the gondola by my head, and I reflected that, if the LS3 was perhaps safe, I nevertheless wasn't.

The great airship rose majestically into the night as I started up the stern engines. A few moments later, the Bolsheviks had dwindled into nothing and the LS3 carried us through the gathering darkness towards safety.

CHAPTER 13
A JOURNEY ACROSS RUSSIA

Arkady Chaikin, the thief who had stolen the Kazanskaya, had stood trial in St. Petersburg, in the north-western part of Russia, and we thought that we might be able to locate him by consulting the records of his trial. Accordingly, Sikorsky and I laid in a heading for St. Petersburg, home of the Winter Palace and seat of the Imperial Government of Russia.

We flew across Russia throughout the next day, and landed outside St. Petersburg shortly after nightfall. Once again, we determined that Fritz would stay on the LS3, while the rest of us would venture into the city.

"We need to find another nurse," said Ari with a sigh. Archie had had a nurse, but she had left when we had discovered that she was an international jewel thief. It seems strange, but that's the sort of thing that happens to us.

After breakfast, Fritz drove us to the edge of the city, where we found a streetcar-stop and waited for it to turn up. The streets were uncannily silent. It was like standing in a cemetery.

Sikorsky shook his head. "Who cleans up here? Who?" he lamented. "This was once most beautiful city in all of Russia! Now, look at it—look at heaps of rubbish, look at filthy pools of water! Who is cleaning up here? Who?"

But nobody felt much like talking as we waited and waited. We were on the point of giving up when we heard the rattle of wheels, and a streetcar rounded a corner and pulled to a stop beside us. A few passengers alighted, their eyes turned firmly downwards, and scattered in all directions. We boarded. The driver shook his reins and the skinny horses heaved the streetcar off. It was packed, and there were no free seats, so we held tight to leather wrist-straps suspended from the ceiling.

Sikorsky jingled change in his pocket and spoke to the conductor, a man with sunken cheeks and eyes and a thin, straggling moustache. The conversation became more heated, until Sikorsky, lips pursed in disgust, handed him some coins in exchange for four tickets.

"Six roubles!" he exploded. "Six!" He lapsed for a few sentences into muttered Russian. "Six roubles, it is . . . " He did a quick mental calculation. "It is twelve shillings. One dollar," he added for Ari's benefit.

"You could travel a long way for a dollar in the States," observed Ari.

"This trip, she is three miles," complained Sikorsky. "Three miserable miles! We could buy car for this much!"

I narrowed my eyes at him. "Don't exaggerate, Vasili Ivanovich," I told him. "The fee is expensive, but it's our only option."

Sikorsky opened his mouth to protest, then remembering his words to me earlier grinned and fell silent.

The streetcar moved through more and more empty streets, stopping occasionally to let off or admit more passengers. Those who disembarked vanished up side-streets or through doors, but they did not linger. Nobody spoke, and few sounds came to us from the streets. Nevertheless, the driver rang his bell at every junction and the sound of the conductor's ticket machine clicked on like distant typing. Sikorsky found a seat next to a lady who appeared to be in her sixties, her grey hair showing beneath the hem of her head scarf. At length, he turned to me and said, "This lady, Marfa Alexeiovna, she says Bolsheviks now control Duma."

"The what?"

"Duma—is men who control Russia, like Parliament or Senate. Duma's rules are very strict now. They say strict rules will continue until Russia is safe from War."

We now passed along city streets, where the buildings towered above us on either side. We emerged into a wide square with a bronze equestrian statue of Nicholas I. On the further side of it rose the gold-plated dome of St. Isaac's Cathedral.

"Winter Palace is that way, though we cannot see it from here," explained Sikorsky, whispering though we hardly knew why. "All the government buildings are nearby. We will find records of Chaikin's trial here, I think."

Just before we reached the cathedral, a woman in a blue uniform, with a rifle slung over her shoulder, held out a hand, palm-outwards, to stop us. Marfa Alexeiovna made the Sign of the Cross. Sikorsky spoke with her again and then told the rest of us: "These blue uniforms—they are the Municipal Police. The people are very afraid of them."

"Are the court buildings far?" I asked.

"*Nyet.*" Sikorsky pointed. "A few hundred yards down there."

"Then let's walk." We clambered down from the streetcar and moved off, but the policewoman waved angrily at us to be still. A moment later, we realized why: a column of soldiers marched into sight, rifles shouldered. They all bore red stars on their fur hats and red flashes on their epaulettes.

After a while, the column came to an end, and Sikorsky led us down the street past the cathedral. Ahead of us, we could see the blue of the Nevsky River; on our right was a wooded park, on our left a yellow building with tall white columns, which Sikorsky explained was the Senate Building. "This is very dangerous place for us," he added. "We must take care."

We came to a massive arch, at which stood a sentry in the blue uniform of the Municipal Police. Beyond the arch lay a cobbled street, flanked by tall buildings. Sikorsky turned to face us. "You have no passports—no Russian passports, at least. I think foreigners will be regarded with suspicion. You would be caught and thrown into jail. I have old passport, but it will be sufficient, I think."

He strode off towards the arch and we watched as the sentry unslung his rifle and demanded his passport. After a brief conversation, the sentry summoned an officer, who examined the passport some more, asked Sikorsky a barrage of questions, and then reluctantly handed the passport back to him. Frowning, he waved Sikorsky past, but watched him suspiciously, his eyes narrowed, his hand resting on the holster of his pistol.

"I think that officer's going to rat on Sikorsky," I observed.

"We need to cause a distraction," suggested Ari.

"Do you have any more tear gas?" I asked.

Ari's brows contracted and she pursed her lips. "That would be dumb," she said.

"I have an idea." We both stared, surprised, for it was Grubworthy who had spoken. He waddled across the street to the arch, waving his British passport at the sentry, and said, "Excuse me, but can you tell me the way to the British Consulate, please?"

Hearing the English, the officer turned away from Sikorsky and towards Grubworthy. He closed in and spoke a few words to him.

"No, no," replied Grubworthy, "I'm afraid I don't speak Russian. But I need to speak with the British Ambassador. Can you direct me to him, please?" After another barrage of Russian, Grubworthy asked, "Is there anyone there who can speak English?" After a pause, he said, "Speaksi Anglyski?"

"*Vy Anglychanin?*" demanded the officer.

"*Da,*" answered Grubworthy. He thrust his thumb at his own chest. "*Anglyski.*" He spread his hands. "British Consulate?"

"*Britanskoye Konsultsvo?*" answered the officer, and Grubworthy nodded with enthusiasm.

"He's better than I am," breathed Ari, awestruck. Meanwhile, Sikorsky had disappeared through one of the doors on the cobbled street. Grubworthy, seeing this out of the corner of his eye, held up his hands in resignation as the officer unleashed a torrent of impassioned Russian at him. He backed off and sauntered away along the street, towards the river. The Russian officer shook his head and strode away in that fashion people have who think they have something more important to do elsewhere.

We walked parallel to Grubworthy for a while on opposite sides of the street, finally joining him at a low stone wall below which flowed the Nevsky River.

"Cadwallader, that was brilliant!" enthused Ari, and I echoed her sentiments.

Grubworthy shrugged. "Well, I can't do much," he responded, "but I know how to be confused."

We waited perhaps half an hour longer before we saw Sikorsky hurrying across the street towards us.

"Did you find out where Chaikin is?" I asked as he joined us.

Sikorsky nodded. "I had to bribe many people, including friend of mine from university. But I found record of Chaikin's trial."

"What happened to him?" asked Ari. "Is he . . . dead?"

"Perhaps, perhaps not." Sikorsky paused a moment to look at the view across the Nevsky, as if he were seeing something he loved for the last time. "At his trial, Chaikin claimed that he sold icon's frame, but left icon itself in monastery in Siberia."

"Are there a lot of monasteries in Siberia?" I asked.

"Many hundreds."

"So where is Chaikin now? Maybe we can ask him."

"He was sent to Akatuy Katorga for ten years' hard labour."

"The what?"

"Katorga is system of labour camps. This one is in Akatuy in Dauria." He shook his head sadly. "Arkady Chaikin was sent there twelve years ago. He may already be dead."

"But we have to go anyway, don't we?" said Ari, and we knew we must.

We did not leave St. Petersburg at once, but stayed through the following day, which was Saturday.

"Oughtn't we to leave at once?" wondered Grubworthy, when we were back in the LS3. "Aren't you afraid Von Krems will get to Chaikin before we do?"

"Is risk," admitted Sikorsky. "But we must go to Mass. There is Catholic Church of St. Catherine on Nevsky Prospect," he concluded.

"But what happens if Von Krems gets ahead of us? Won't he get to the thief before we can?"

"Relax, Grubworthy," I told him. "We're in an airship. They have to rely on trains and cars. We'll be way ahead of them."

"It's important to get to Mass," Ari concluded, "even if it puts us at a disadvantage."

So, over Grubworthy's protests, we stayed an extra day in St. Petersburg, went to Mass on Sunday morning, and took off for Siberia directly afterwards.

That was the beginning of the longest trip I think we've ever taken in the LS3. Mostly what rolled past beneath us was cornfields, now beginning the harvest. Nothing much happened on this journey, except that Edison went missing, and we pulled the LS3 apart until we discovered him on top of one of the wheels of the Daimler. A few nights later, Grubworthy woke us all up by screaming suddenly in fear. Everybody clattered along the corridor to his cabin, where we found him sitting bolt upright in bed, shaking all over.

"I've had the most awful dream," he confessed after our urgent inquiries. "I dreamed that the Devil came to get my soul."

"Oh, Cadwallader, that's awful!" Ari sympathized.

"I asked him if there was any food in Hell, and he said, Yes, there was. So I said I'd be happy to go along." He downed the glass of water Fritz had handed him. "Well, that lasted about a week. Then the Devil came to me and said, 'I'm running out of food for the other devils, Cadwallader. I'm afraid you'll have to go to Limbo, you'll have to go to Limbo.' And there wasn't any food at all in Limbo!"

I didn't notice, however, that his appetite was particularly impaired by his dream; the next day he devoured as much as ever, or perhaps even more, at breakfast, and then again at lunch. It was as if he were stockpiling food so as to be able to survive Limbo.

Meanwhile, the days stretched endlessly as we passed over deep forests, lonely lakes and winding rivers, then over jagged snow-capped mountains. Six days we flew on, then dropped to two hundred feet and skimmed over the deep green spear-heads of a pine forest. Sikorsky consulted his navigation charts, the sextant, and the compass, adjusting our course minutely. At length, there appeared in the forward windows of the wheelhouse a pale green clearing in the forest, in the middle of which rested the grey smudge of a small town. Akatuy lay in a wide bowl of flat land surrounded by distant mountains. It was nothing more than a collection of houses along a single street and the prison camp, its grim buildings surrounded by a whitewashed wall.

"It shouldn't be too difficult to land here," I observed.

Suddenly, Sikorsky cried out in surprise and pointed. On the flat grassy steppe below us was an aeroplane. Sikorsky throttled down the engines and turned up all the flaps. The LS3 began an almost vertical descent. Fritz hurried out of the wheelhouse to cast out the anchors. A few moments later, the great airship was stationary, its gondola only ten feet from the grey grass of Siberia, flattened by the stiff wind that howled in from the steppe. Fritz and I turned a crank in the carriage house and lowered the ramp.

This was perhaps the loneliest place on earth. The pine forests all around and the lonely flat steppe on which we had landed looked as if no living thing had ever visited them. The village was not far off, but there was no sign of humanity there at all. It was like a ghost town. We moved away from the LS3 like ants crawling across the moon.

Twenty yards away stood the aeroplane Sikorsky had spotted. It was huge, with a wingspan that must have been almost a hundred feet and four Sunbeam 150 horsepower engines. Its blunt nose was almost all glass, but otherwise there was but a single window port and starboard about halfway down the fuselage.

"It is Ilya Muromets," exclaimed Sikorsky in wonder. He ran his hand over the leading edge of the lower wing. "Is designed by my cousin, Igor. He work on it right after helping me with Russky Vityaz."

"It's a military plane," I said, pointing at the Imperial insignia on the tail.

"It was designed for passengers, but has been used for bombing."

"What is it doing here?" wondered Grubworthy.

"I think I know," I answered him, "but let's make certain." Reaching up, I pulled open the hatch and hoisted myself onboard. Sikorsky followed.

"Mac, is this a good idea?" asked Ari, looking up at us through the hatch, Archie on her hip.

"This is a very good idea," I answered her. "And it will help."

The interior was one large, narrow compartment, with easy chairs bolted to the floor in the stern and a wheelhouse surprisingly like the LS3's in the bows, except that there was a seat for the pilot. A table was fixed to the floor between the easy chairs, and on it lay several books and pieces of paper, some of which were written in Russian, some in German.

"That clinches it," I said. "Von Krems is here."

"I knew you shouldn't have gone to church," whined Grubworthy.

But before I could speak, Ari's voice came from outside, calling my name. There was a tremor in her voice, which I knew signaled danger. Sikorsky, Grubworthy and I all looked out, to see a crowd of people fanned out around the hatch. They were mainly Bolshevik soldiers, but at the centre stood Von Krems, now with his arm in a sling as well as his head bandaged. Next to him stood Rabotnik, who held by the elbow a small man with wild, grey hair and sunken cheeks.

"Chaikin?" I asked, and the small man nodded, his eyes wide with fear.

The soldiers all had their rifles aimed directly at us.

"Welcome to Siberia, Herr McCracken," sneered Von Krems.

CHAPTER 14
FINDING THE SIBERIAN MONASTERY

Von Krems had brought with him four Bolshevik soldiers; probably the aeroplane could not carry more passengers than that. I raised my hands to show I was unarmed and slowly stepped down onto the wiry grass. "How are you doing, Rabotnik?" I nodded towards the man he held. Fear was scrawled over his features. "And you must be Arkady Chaikin. I'm glad to meet you. So, Franz, are you going to kill us?"

"Fortunately for you," replied Von Krems, "I have no orders to do so. Sufficient it will be simply to prevent you from following us. And, let us say, I wish that you live, so that you may see our great cause succeed."

My eyes dropped to Von Krems' sling. "Did you hurt yourself falling from that wrecking ball, Franz? We've met twice, and you've had two injuries. And here we are again."

"The time for witticisms is not now, Herr McCracken," Von Krems sneered. "Humour is such a decadent western vice."

"It's difficult to be as serious as a communist." Sikorsky and Grubworthy were at my back now. "But surely you haven't fallen for all that communist rubbish, have you, Count Franz August Kunstler Von Krems?"

"Once again, Herr McCracken, your humour fails to hit the mark. You wish to insult me by reminding me of my noble birth. But I have since leaving Austria renounced my title, and put all my family's fortune at the service of Herr Lenin. Yes, it was the money formerly belonging to my family that financed Comrade Lenin's return to Russia." His smile flashed briefly through the mask of his face, like a lighthouse glimpsed briefly through fog. "You see, I am wholly committed to the cause. The time for the aristocrats is over—it is useless to pretend otherwise. This War has finished them off. There is no strength left in the monarchies of Europe." He glanced briefly at Ari. "Or in the supposed Republic of America, which will soon be communist as well. No one will stand before us. Communism is the only way forward for the human race." Turning to one of the soldiers, he spoke haltingly in broken Russian. The soldier ran off towards the LS3.

"I saw the faces of the people in St. Petersburg," I said. "Fear, paranoia, starvation—is that truly the future of the human race under communism?"

There came a flash of discomfort behind the eyes, but oddly enough, not behind Von Krems'—it was Rabotnik's eyes that changed so briefly. But Von Krems spoke, and I couldn't think about Rabotnik for a moment. "I suppose you believe the hope of the world lies in your antiquated religion," he countered. "You have had nineteen hundred years. Christianity has been tried and found wanting."

"On the contrary," retorted Ari, "it's been found difficult and left untried."

A gunshot rang out, followed by the sound of liquid gushing onto the ground. The soldier had shot a hole in one of the LS3's engines.

The left corner of Von Krems' mouth twitched upward in a humourless smile. "Christianity is difficult, Frau McCracken, but communism is easy. It is an obvious solution to the world's problems. What is so difficult to understand? We will take care of you. If you need food, the government will give it to you. If you need shelter, the government will give it to you. If you need an education, the government will give it to you."

Ari's eyes dropped for a moment to Archie, whom she still clutched in her arms. "What of the family?" she asked.

"From the present, it still has its uses," replied Von Krems, "but it is antiquated, like religion." Another gunshot echoed across the steppe. Von Krems went on, "Do not fear, Frau McCracken, we will in the end eradicate the family, so that all good will come from the social structure, a social structure constructed by those with the wisdom to do it. Even you, Frau McCracken, will one day admit that you love your government more than your husband or your son." He gave a twisted sort of smile. "How does the phrase go, Who can do more for you—the master or the servant? The government can do more for you than your husband. It will be a kind of big brother."

"There's only one real Brother, Von Krems," returned Ari with her typical frostiness. "You're not Him and neither is Lenin." A third gunshot rang out and we had only one engine left.

Von Krems sighed. "In the end, you see, all talk is useless. Action is all. The strong arm in every conflict will the word defeat. And the practical situation is that we have Herr Chaikin and his information. We have an aeroplane. We will this ridiculous object of superstition find and destroy, and you will be powerless to stop us, however many words you use." A fourth gunshot seemed to provide a period to his sentence. "I know that you can repair the engines of your airship, Herr McCracken. But by that time, we will be from you a very long way indeed. There will be no possibility to follow us. You have lost the trail of this magic picture." The soldier returned and once again leveled his rifle at us. "*Auf wiedersehen*, Herr McCracken." Von Krems pushed past me and up to the aeroplane's hatch. Turning, he said thoughtfully, "You know, there is part of me that admires you. The only real enemy of human progress is the supernatural. You cannot oppose physical force with physical force. If that were so, this War would have been very successful. The only real enemies of communism are the Church and the family. I admire you as I admire a great enemy. But be under no illusions. We will win. It is our destiny." He reached up the handrail to pull himself into the plane. As he did so, however, his foot slipped on a rung and his chin hit the metal frame of the hatch.

"Three," I said.

Von Krems unleashed a stream of German at me, at which Ari and Fritz cocked an eyebrow. But then Von Krems was in the plane. The soldiers began embarking, and one of them appeared in the pilot's seat. Another of them stepped up to one of the propellers and spun it. The engine caught and he went on to the next propeller.

Rabotnik climbed into the plane, yanking Chaikin with him.

At the last moment, just before Chaikin disappeared into the aeroplane, he looked at us with his wild eyes and shouted, "Por-Bazhyn! Por-Bazhyn!" One of the soldiers turned instantly and slammed the butt of his rifle into Chaikin's stomach. Ari cried out in alarm. But Rabotnik just grabbed him by the scruff of the neck and dragged him roughly, coughing and writhing, into the aircraft.

It was then I remembered what I had been trying to recall: the tattoo of the crucifix on Rabotnik's neck, and I wondered what to make of it and his odd expression just now.

"What does Por-Bazhyn mean, I wonder?" asked Ari.

"I hope it's a place-name," I answered.

By now, all four engines, six hundred horsepower, were screaming, and we all backed away from the aeroplane. The last soldier hopped up through the hatch and slammed it closed behind him. The pilot gunned the engines and the aircraft surged forward, taxiing away from us. The wheels bumped over hillocks and molehills. Then the flaps moved and the great aeroplane lifted off and soared into the air. It circled us once, dipped its wing as if in a mock salute, then flew off into the west, leaving us alone in Siberia.

"Sikorsky," I said, "I'll make a damage report if you'll find this Por-Bazhyn place on the charts and lay in a course."

Sikorsky dashed off to do just that, the others following him, while I took a look at the damage to the engines. It was mostly repairable. The casing of the two stern engines was simply punctured, and all I had to do was weld a new piece of steel over the bullet-holes. But in one of the forward engines, the bullet had knocked a piston out of alignment; in the other, the bullet had nicked one of the propeller blades. I knew I could get the stern engines working quickly, and that I could repair the piston and machine a new propeller blade in our workshop while we were in flight, so after my inspection, I returned to the LS3.

Entering the gondola, the first thing I saw was Archie, with the cat under one arm. "Where are you going?" I asked.

"Put-a cat-a oven," he answered in a businesslike fashion, toddling off towards the galley. "Put-a cat-a oven. Put-a cat-a oven."

A moment later, Ari rattled down the steps from the upper level. "Have you seen Archie?"

I nodded. "He was with Edison," I said. "He told me he was going to put him in the oven. I think you'll find him in the galley."

"He's doing what?" Ari raced after Archie and Edison while I sauntered to the navigation room, where I found Sikorsky poring over a map of Siberia. He shrugged sadly upon seeing me.

"I can find nothing like Por-Bazhyn on these maps. Chaikin was from Tuva, which is close to border with Mongolia. It is about eight hundred miles. So I make assumption that he leave icon in monastery in Tuva. But there is no Por-Bazhyn." I explained the situation with the engines. "Is good," he said. "When I know where we go, we can take off. With only two engines, we will fly at half speed, but is better than nothing. Von Krems will get very far ahead."

"But he'll have to refuel, won't he?"

"*Da.*" Sikorsky brightened a little. "He has no spare fuel in Muromets. Refueling will take him off course. We have fuel to reach Tuva, perhaps not to get back to Europe afterwards."

"No!" came Archie's protesting voice from the passageway outside. "No no no no *no*!" A moment later, Ari joined us, Archie, red-faced, on her hip.

"Will you explain to your son that he's not to put the cat in the oven?" she said.

"It sounds to me like you've explained that already," I answered. Her eyes flashed. "Okay, I'll try." I took Archie from her and turned his face towards mine. "Archie, you can't put cats in ovens. You can't eat cats."

"Put-a cat-a oven," answered Archie sullenly.

"I know you think cats are an incarnation of evil, but they're for playing with, not putting in ovens."

"Cat evil," said Archie. "Put-a cat-a oven."

"He may have a point," I admitted to Ari.

"No he doesn't." Ari was annoyed now. "Archie, you can't put Edison into the oven. Mama says no. All right?"

It wasn't all right with Archie, but he had to admit defeat. Mother had spoken. He buried his face in my shoulder and rubbed his eyes. "How did he get away from you?" I asked.

"While you were inspecting the engines," Ari explained, "I was reading in the library. I stopped paying attention for a moment." She looked at the map. "Did you find Por-Bazhyn?"

"Perhaps you shouldn't read when you're supposed to be looking after Archie," I said in a very quiet voice so that maybe Ari wouldn't hear me.

Ari's eyes flashed again as she looked at me sidelong, but then she redirected her attention to the map.

"Por-Bazhyn is not on map," confessed Sikorsky.

"We know three things," explained Ari. We both gave her our full attention, including Archie, whose attention comprised in trying to wriggle out of my arms.

I set him down. "No putting the cat in the oven, Archie, all right?"

Archie nodded without making any promises and toddled off down the passageway.

"What we know," said Ari, counting the items off on her fingers, "is, first, that Von Krems and the others headed west. Second, we know that Chaikin is from Tuva, and that in Tuva the main language is one of the Turkic languages. Since our trip to Zun a few years ago, I've become pretty familiar with the Turkic languages. Third, we know that Chaikin left the icon in a monastery.'"

"So we're looking for a monastery in Tuva called Por-Bazhyn?"

Ari nodded. We all bent over the map, but could make out nothing. At last, I straightened. "So what do we do?"

Sikorsky answered my question. "We take off, we fly towards Tuva." He unfolded another map, drawing an invisible line with his finger across the eastern portion of Russia. "This flight will take us maybe two days. By then, Ari will have solution, no?"

Ari didn't answer at once. She looked at the map a long time. Finally, she said, "By God's grace I shall."

We took off from Akatuy just an hour later, the tiny village sliding away from us slowly as we crawled on two engines over the ground we had just covered. I spent the afternoon knocking the piston back into shape, and had just fastened the cowling back on when Fritz appeared on the gantry nearby. The wind whipped his red hair and his clothes, and he grasped the railing tightly as he cupped his other hand about his mouth.

"Herr McCracken!" he shouted. "Dinner is served in the *Speiseraum*."

I gathered up my tools and followed him back into the gondola, stepping out of my fleece-lined overalls and hanging them on a hook near the door. I could hear voices in the dining room already, and a wonderful aroma flowed through the doorway to fill me with delight and remind me of how hungry I had become whilst repairing the engine.

Dinner that evening consisted of what Fritz called *pelmeni*, tasty little dumplings containing pork, beef and onions, with a salad of cucumbers, onions and tomatoes tossed in red wine and herbs, and a wonderful bread stuffed with fruit, honey, and cinnamon. We ate as if we'd starved for months, particularly Grubworthy.

"Don't worry, Grubworthy," I said, biting into one of the *pelmeni* so that the explosion of flavour filled my mouth. Grubworthy turned towards me as I savoured the pork and beef for a few moments. "We'll be back in England before too long—at least before the New Year."

Grubworthy considered a moment. "Oh, I wasn't thinking about that." He spread a slice of the fruit bread with butter and bit off a piece. "I was just thinking about Von Krems and what he said."

"You mean all that rot about communism?"

"Well, it's not entirely rot, if you think about it."

"Yes it is."

Ari's brow wrinkled. "What do you mean, Cadwallader?" She was cutting up some of the *pelmeni* for Archie.

Grubworthy spent a moment in reflection. "Well, it's not so very different from Christianity, is it? It's looking after the poor."

My jaw moved a couple of times, but I couldn't think of a reply. Fortunately, Ari was ready with one. "Looking after the poor is only part of the Christian life," she explained. "Communism misses all the rest. It isn't real charity. When you force people to be generous, it isn't the real thing. The Church doesn't force you to look after the poor. It's something you do freely, out of love."

"But it's close, surely."

"It's missing something crucial," Ari explained patiently. "It's missing freedom and love. And something that's been good, but has had parts of it taken away or distorted—well, that's practically a definition of *evil*. Communism makes the government do what the family and the religious orders should be doing out of love."

Grubworthy gave a few slow nods. "I see," he said. "But what if you don't have a family? What if your father left you when you were very small, and you can barely remember him? And all you get is a Christmas card every year or two? Who can look after you then? Not the Church—not my church, anyway. It would have to be the government."

"Oh, Cadwallader!" Ari's eyes welled with tears. But none of us could think of anything to say.

For a few moments, Grubworthy watched Archie eating his *pelmeni*, then he said, "You know, I really like the way you take your little boy on adventures with you." He seemed to regain his energy and resumed his dinner with vigour. "The closest thing I've ever had to a family," he said, "is what I've found on this airship."

He was quite surprised, a second or two later, to find Ari's arms flung around his neck.

We flew on through the night and through the next day while I worked on the propeller of the fourth engine. Finally, I got the new blade fitted and inserted the hand crank. It was a little stiff turning, and I realized that the starter gear was frozen. I looked in frustration along the body of the LS3 at the working motors. The LS3 cruised over the Sayan Mountains at about 5,000 feet above sea level, and the peaks below us were all solid snow. The stern engines were in perfect working condition because they had kept warm by working constantly, whereas the forward engines had been idle and therefore cold. It would be a while before I could warm them up and get them working again. Resignedly, I packed up all my tools and went back inside, explaining the situation to Sikorsky.

"Is another problem. Look." I followed Sikorsky's extended finger through the forward windows and saw that dark clouds were gathering in the west ahead of us. "Is first snowfall," Sikorsky explained. "It comes early this year. It will make things more difficult."

"Well, we'll just have to beat the snow, if we can," I said.

Sikorsky nodded. "On just two engines," he pointed out in that irritatingly gloomy Russian way he had.

Rubbing the warmth back into my hands, I climbed the stairs to the top deck and, not finding Ari in our cabin, opened the door to the library, where I found her poring over several books, a lamp pooling yellow light on her desk.

"Any progress?" I asked.

She looked up, startled, for she had not hear my approach. "Well, I found out that in Tuvan, Por Bazhyn means 'clay house.'"

"Is that important?"

"Most people in Tuva build in timber—a clay house would be unusual. But why call it a house when it's a monastery? That's what I don't understand."

I flipped over one of the books on the desk, without losing her place. It was called *A Grammar and Lexicon of the Ancient Turkish Languages.* She had borrowed it three years ago, I recalled, when we had flown to the Land of Zun on a previous adventure.

"What are Turks doing in Siberia anyway?" I wondered.

"They're a Turkish people called the Uyghurs," Ari explained. "They've been there for over a thousand years. And not just in Tuva—in China too.

They live in China, but they look just like Turks you'd see on the streets of Istanbul."

"And they're Christian?" I asked. At Ari's puzzled look, I went on, "Well, monasteries are Christian, aren't they? There aren't Muslim monasteries, are there?"

"No, there aren't any Muslim monasteries," agreed Ari, "but Islam isn't the only religion in Tuva—there are a few Christians, but most of the people are Buddhists. And Buddhists have monasteries."

"So Chaikin could have left the icon in a Buddhist monastery?"

"I suppose so," agreed Ari, "but I can't find one called Por-Bazhyn at all." She gave a sigh, rubbed her eyes, and rested her face in her hands for a moment. "How long until we reach Tuva?"

"Tomorrow morning," I replied. Ari said nothing more, and I left the library, returning to the wheelhouse. Sikorsky glanced over his shoulder at me.

"We have heading?"

I shook my head. But a moment later, Ari's voice came over the speaking tube. "Vasili, Mac, can you find a village called Kungurtuk on the charts?"

Sikorsky leaped over to the table at the back of the wheelhouse and scanned the map. His brow was furrowed but, as if reading his thoughts, Ari's voice added: "Try near the border with Mongolia."

"I have it!"

"There should be a lake, about five miles west of it."

"Lake Tere-Khol?"

"That's the one. Just a moment. I'll be right there."

Sikorsky went into a frenzy of activity, scribbling numbers on a piece of paper, drawing lines with a ruler on the chart, and consulting various instruments. In the middle of all this, Ari appeared in the doorway, her eyes red-rimmed with weariness but a smile upon her lips.

"How did you find it?" I asked.

"It was the Uyghurs," she answered. "I should have known. I just looked up the history of the Uyghurs, and found that one of their khans, Moyanchur, married a princess of the Chinese Tang Dynasty called Ninguo. He built a palace in the Chinese style, to make her feel at home."

"So it was a palace, not a monastery?"

"No, it was abandoned soon after Moyanchur's death. His son Tengri became khan after him, but when he decided to invade China to take control of the Silk Road, his uncle Bagha murdered him and two thousand of his family and followers."

"Two thousand!" I gave a long whistle. "That was a busy day."

"Well, Bagha Khan found he couldn't live in a palace where he'd had two thousand people put to death, so he gave it to the Manicheans for a monastery. Later on, it became a Buddhist monastery, but it hasn't ever been inhabited for long at a stretch since the massacre. It was discovered less than thirty years ago, which is why it isn't on the maps."

At sunrise the day after, we descended between green mountains towards the little village of Kungurtuk. It occupied a flat space of about a square mile near the confluence of two rivers and consisted mainly of log cabins with large corrals adjoining them. The two rivers, having rushed from the mountains into this valley, dashed off southwards, and it was this river we now followed.

Ice had begun to form on the forward windows, and snowflakes rushed towards us. Winter had begun in Siberia.

Another twenty minutes of following the river, and it opened up into a wide lake, the edges of which had frozen over for about a quarter of mile.

On one of these wide margins of ice stood the Ilya Muromets. Von Krems had reached Por-Bazhyn ahead of us.

CHAPTER 15
INTO THE PIT

Sikorsky immediately spun the wheel and the LS3 turned its nose ponderously eastwards. Ari and I dashed to the starboard windows. An island lay below us, the ruins of a fortress laid out on it as on an architect's blueprints, and the plane stood on the ice beside it. Around us were mountains, but unlike further north, the shores of the lake were entirely treeless. There seemed to be nowhere to hide.

"How did they get here before us?" I demanded.

Sikorsky righted the wheel and the LS3 arrested its turn, flying straight from the lake a while. "We have only two engines, they have four."

"Do you think they saw us?" wondered Ari. "I don't see anyone around."

"Perhaps they're all in the monastery," I suggested.

"It's probably harder than you think," observed Grubworthy, "sneaking up on someone in an airship."

"We can't do anything but go on," I answered.

The ground below us was not flat, but undulated like waves on the sea. We could see patches of snow between the long grass, which was flattened by a stiff breeze. Sikorsky eased the nose of the LS3 down-wards and the grass rose to meet us. The lake slid from view behind a grassy rise. Chains rattled and anchors dropped fore and aft. Sikorsky cut the engines. We could hear the wind soughing through the wiry grass of the steppe.

It took a while to get into cold weather gear and then to gather weapons from the armoury on the LS3's top deck. When we had snaked down the rope ladder to the iron-hard ground below, we stood like explorers on the moon, gaping at our surroundings and wondering what to do next.

Climbing to the top of the rise, we peered over its crest towards the lake. Por-Bazhyn was roughly square in plan and about a hundred and eighty yards along each side. The outer wall, though jagged at the top, effectively screened the interior from our eyes, except that a dome did show itself above the battlements.

"That's Por-Bazhyn," said Ari cheerfully. "What do you think, Archie? Por-Bazhyn?"

"Pubby shin, pubby shin," repeated Archie to himself.

"I still don't see anyone," I said, passing my binoculars to Sikorsky. "Perhaps they're all inside. I would have expected someone to be guarding the plane, though."

Sikorsky stared through the binoculars. "If they do not expect us," he reasoned, "they may not take usual care. No guard in aeroplane is good—perhaps it means they miss our approach." Lowering the binoculars, I could see his eyes shone. "Let us find this icon, for Holy Russia!"

We all made the Sign of the Cross. In addition, Fritz cocked his Mauser.

Swarming over the rise and down the other side, we felt our faces stung by icy wind from the lake, bringing with it flakes of snow. Archie cried a little in surprise, but Ari held him close and he quieted down.

In a few moments, we had crossed the narrow margin of ice and were passing the aeroplane. We all gathered in its shadow, while the snow flurries spun around us. Sikorsky and I reached up and tried the door. It opened outwards, creaking a little. I sprang up, my revolver at the ready. But the plane was empty.

"We might steal their fuel," I said, pointing at the petrol cans crowded into the stern of the fuselage.

"We should sabotage plane, so they cannot escape with Blessed Virgin."

I nodded and looked around for some instruments of mischief. Strapped behind the pilot's seat was a toolbox, and we took a hammer and a pair of wire-cutters. Jumping down from the plane, Sikorsky tapped on one of the propeller blades while I snipped some of the bracing wires.

Ari's brow was deeply furrowed. "You don't want to kill them, do you?"

"The pilot will notice problems during his pre-flight check," I answered. "This will just slow them down a bit."

"I think we should be going now," Ari pointed out.

I nodded. The entrance to the monastery stood before us, and a little off to the left, but the gates had long since rotted, leaving a wide opening. We flattened ourselves against the wall and peeked through the opening.

Most of the interior was in ruins, nothing but a series of low walls. But rising above them stood a building that seemed to have been used more recently. Circular in design and with a domed roof, the building stood at the centre of the monastery like the only important thing in the world.

"That's a *stupa*," whispered Ari. "It's a kind of Buddhist shrine—it's where they keep the relics of old monks."

"Like a mausoleum?"

"A little, but it's also a shrine—pilgrims would visit a stupa."

"Tupa," said Archie. "Tupa dupa bupa mupa."

I looked again. An open space, most likely a courtyard, lay between us and the stupa, but there was plenty of fallen masonry to act as cover. And no one seemed to be around.

We all dashed across the courtyard. Halfway across, Ari stooped and picked up a small object. When we climbed some shallow steps to reach the door of the stupa, she held out a yellowish rock to me. It was circular, and had a concentric design stamped into one end.

"Clay," said Ari. "Chinese style. That's why this place is called 'clay-house.'"

The door was painted red, though the paint had been flaking for decades, and sported a golden door-knocker in the middle. I thought it was fashioned to look like one of those dogs who look as if someone has pressed their noses in, but Ari told me later it was really a Chinese dragon.

The door was ajar.

Peering around it, I was initially confronted by impenetrable darkness. But as my eyes grew accustomed to the dimness of the interior, I saw the lavishly decorated walls, much decayed now, the statue of Buddha, the doors opposite us and to each side. Light filtered into the large space through a crack in the ceiling that ran from one side to the other, illuminating the central feature of the stupa, which was a wide pillar that joined the ceiling with the floor. The more I looked at it, the more I saw that it was supposed to remind the observer of a tree, with leafy branches radiating out along the ceiling and roots depicted in mosaics on the floor.

In front of the pillar, staring at a crack in the ground—that in the ceiling continued across the wide floor—stooped Von Krems, Rabotnik and Chaikin.

"Do they have the icon?" asked Grubworthy in a whisper so loud it virtually echoed.

I flashed him a warning look and whispered back: "They wouldn't be here if they had."

"Where are the soldiers?"

"I don't know, Grubworthy. Searching other parts of the monastery? Obviously they aren't in here."

"I don't like it." Grubworthy folded his arms over his chest. "I think we should find out what the soldiers are doing."

I opened my mouth to reply, then snapped it shut again. He was right—Grubworthy was learning much about adventures! "All right," I consented. "Sikorsky, you, Grubworthy and Fritz go and search the rest of the ruins for the soldiers. Ari and I will confront Von Krems. Don't split up—there's safety in numbers."

"Ready?" I said to Ari, when the others had slunk off on their adventure. She gave a nod. All three of us marched into the stupa, Archie holding his mother's free hand. I had my revolver out and pointing at Von Krems.

"The game's up, Von Krems," I called out as we drew near.

180

Hearing my voice, the three men looked up at us. There was no surprise in their faces. Chaikin still looked afraid. Von Krems smiled. "Quite right, Herr McCracken." It was hard for him to talk, as his chin had been heavily bandaged since the last time we had seen him. "For you, the game really is up."

Von Krems reached for his holster, but I leveled my gun and thumbed back the hammer. "Are you mad?" I demanded. "We've already got you covered."

"At the risk of sounding decadently theatrical, Herr McCracken," sniggered Von Krems, "look behind you."

I cast a glance over my shoulder. The doorway darkened a moment, as a troop of people entered: the four Bolshevik soldiers. They had captured and disarmed Fritz, Sikorsky, and Grubworthy. Fritz was bleeding from the head; Grubworthy's eye was puffing up and already discoloured. One of the Russians held Fritz's Mauser at his head; the other three aimed their rifles at the captives or us.

Von Krems gave a laugh. "Really, Herr McCracken," he said, stepping over the crack in the floor to pull my revolver from my hand, "you cannot in an airship expect to go unnoticed."

Rabotnik joined him with a dull laugh. In his hand, the cannonball seemed very small indeed. Chaikin cringed beside his feet, like a whipped dog.

Pocketing my revolver, Von Krems cast a glance over his shoulder and gestured at the treelike pillar behind him with his free hand. "Of all the extraordinary things, Herr McCracken, do you know what this is?"

"The World Tree," Ari answered, "the *Axis Mundi*, the Centre of the World. It represents the tree under which Buddha sat to gain wisdom. They believe that all things in the world turn about the World Tree."

"*Jawohl*, Frau McCracken." Von Krems snapped his heels together and gave her a curt bow. "You would have made a wonderful University professor."

"I take that as an insult," replied Ari.

"*Sehr gut*," answered Von Krems. He walked a few steps back towards the World Tree. Stopping, he turned and said, "Such superstitious nonsense, is it not? Look at this." He gestured at the decorated walls, the statues, the World Tree. "All this labour, all this capital investment, and for what? For a superstition. The centre of the world is not here. From this moment on, the centre of the world is Red Square, Moscow."

"Really," I said. "So now the World Tree is in Red Square? That's the problem with you wallopers: for you, politics is a religion. You should get yourself a real religion, not one of these fake ones."

Von Krems returned to me slowly, his eyes fixed upon mine. "Look around you, Herr McCracken," he advised. "Is this something living you see here? Is it something current? No one has worshiped here for centuries. Religion is dead, Herr McCracken—at least politics lives." He smiled as pleasantly as he could, given the heavy bandaging on his jaw. "The revolution has begun, you see. You may not be aware of this, as you have been in your airship so long, but events in the world are moving along. One week ago, Bolshevik forces captured the Winter Palace in St. Petersburg. The takeover has been complete. Russia is superstitious no longer—now she is communist! From now on, it remains only to spread the good news of communism to the rest of the world." His smile broadened, but it evidently gave him pain. "You see, Herr McCracken, we are the evangelists of the new order. Before long Comrade Lenin, not some starry-eyed philosopher, not some long-dead middle-eastern carpenter, will be the supreme personality in the world."

"If you were certain of that, you wouldn't be here," I pointed out.

With a lightning-fast movement, Von Krems brought the back of his hand crashing into my face. Taken unawares, I was cast to the floor of the stupa, lights flashing before my eyes. Leaning over me so that I could feel his breath upon my forehead, he hissed: "Do not make the mistake of underestimating me, Herr McCracken. I am here to destroy your faith. I will not rest until all religions of the world have been pounded into dust—Buddhism, Christianity, Islam, Judaism, it matters not to me. They must all go! They are all enemies of the new order." Regaining a little composure, he straightened and walked away from me again. "The work of dismantling the superstitions of the past must still be carried out, of course, and that is my glorious duty." Turning, a thoughtful look came over his face. "Has it never occurred to you, Herr McCracken, that your Nazarene prophet made quite the wrong choice in the desert?"

"He did what?"

"Come, come, Herr McCracken, must I teach you your catechism? When the Nazarene went into the desert, he was tempted by the one you call the Evil One. 'If you are the Son of God, command this stone to become bread.' Your so-called saviour's response? 'Man cannot live on bread alone.'" Von Krems shook his head not quite mockingly. "How poorly he understood the human race he claimed to have created! He offered them freedom, when bread was all they wanted. We communists will give the people bread. We will make them happy. Everything they need we will supply to them."

"Men need truth," I responded hotly. I got back onto my feet. "Bread isn't enough."

"*Ja, ja*, this have I heard. 'The truth will set you free.' You see how learned a scholar in your religion I am, Herr McCracken? But I repeat: most men do not wish to be free. Give them food, entertain them with sports and vaudeville shows, and they will be happy. What is the phrase of the Romans? Bread and circuses. Freedom is too much of a burden. They do not want it. Your saviour's solution was too difficult, too unrealistic." Von Krems beat himself on the chest. "We will accept this challenge. We will take on the burden of freedom, so that the people will not have to. We will give them their bread and circuses."

"So have all you communists become bakers now?" It was Ari who had spoken. "Or will Lenin make bread come from the sky, like the manna in the desert?"

Von Krems chuckled with amusement. "*Sehr gut*, Frau McCracken. What a wit you have!"

"I see," said Ari. "You'll force the people to make bread, take it away from them and give it back, and they'll be happy."

Von Krems shrugged. "Of course. Because it is not merely bread—we will take bread from the bakers and give it to the dairy farmers, and milk from the dairy-farmers, which we will give to the bakers. There will be no poverty, no hunger. Who would under these circumstances be unhappy?"

"That's just slavery, Von Krems," I observed. "It isn't real happiness."

Von Krems thought about that for a brief moment. "Perhaps not, but I do not think they will care. I think most people with the illusion of happiness will be content. And you see, Herr McCracken, communism is of the human race a much more realistic appraisal than that of the Nazarene."

"But it won't work," said Ari. "It's not the state's duty to provide food. That's a father's job. You would have the government do what should be done by a family. A mother, a father, a child, that's the image of truth, the image of freedom. Will you destroy that too?"

"We will be the mother and father to the people, Frau McCracken. Is that so very unreasonable? For the family there will be no need, as for God also there will be no need. Truth will come from us, from the Communist Party. And we will tell the truth that will make the people happy. Nothing else is really important." Again he smiled. "I expect you had wondered how you might help us."

"That question's been troubling me for a long time," I said with some irony.

"Ha ha ha. How funny you always are, Herr McCracken. Truly it is said, a Scottish joke is no laughing matter." Von Krems gestured with his Luger towards the crack in the floor. "When from the Law he ran, Chaikin the icon dropped into this crack to dispose of it. He hoped to sell only the frame. Am I correct, Chaikin?"

Chaikin looked fearfully up at him but said nothing. He could understand no English, of course.

"This is what he has to us related. The last vestige of the Russia of superstition down there lies, Herr McCracken, and it is for you to climb down and bring it up."

"So you can destroy it?"

"*Jawohl*, Herr McCracken."

"Why can't you do it yourself? Or send one of your slaves after it?"

"Because I relish the irony of sending you to participate in the eradication of religion from Russia."

"And why would I agree to do something so stupid?"

Von Krems looked as if this was the most idiotic question he had ever heard. "Because if I have not the icon in fifteen minutes, Frau McCracken I will shoot."

My eyes shot over to Ari. She raised her eyes to heaven and said, "Not again."

"Dinna ye folk ever think of anythin' original?" I demanded, rounding on Von Krems. "It's jus' shoot him, shoot her, shoot, shoot, shoot. You just want tae shoot everyone in the world so there's only yersael' left. Then you'll likely shoot yersael'. A' right, a' right, I'll gae—I'd need tae get the icon anyhoo."

A moment of silence followed my outburst, and I saw that the crew of the LS3 was staring at me, wide-eyed. "What did you just say, Mac?" asked Ari.

I shook my head. "It disna matter. I'll go and get the icon."

They had already looped a knotted rope around the bole of the World Tree and let it down into the darkness. I tested the knot securing the rope to the Tree to ensure it was safe, my mind working furiously. Was there some way I could get the icon within fifteen minutes and still prevent Von Krems from destroying it?

From my pocket I drew out my electric torch, flipped the switch, and shone the beam down through the crack. Dimly, at the bottom of whatever was below, I could see piles and piles of pale sticks and smooth boulders.

I strode over to Ari, kissed her and Archie, and said, "I'll be back in less than fifteen minutes." Turning to Von Krems, I added, "It's comforting to know that at the centre of the world lies not *The Communist Manifesto* but an image of a mother and child—*the* Mother and Child." And seizing the knotted rope, I swung myself through the fissure and into the darkness.

I dropped through the dark, my hands working quickly to lower myself from one thick knot to the next. The darkness seemed to wrap itself about me like a thick, clammy blanket. The damp wetness seeped into my soul, and only my frantic desire to find the icon fast and save my family burned like a warm coal at my very centre. My feet touched something and, with a dry rattling, I reached the bottom of wherever I was. I let go of the rope, and found it was difficult to stand upright. The sticks kept shifting under my weight, so that I had to move continually to keep my balance. Taking out my electric torch, I shone it directly on the floor at my feet.

Instantly, I felt my gorge rise. I fell to my knees, retching. They weren't sticks and boulders I was standing in the exact middle of a circular chamber about fifty feet in diameter, and the entire place was full of human bones and skulls. I trembled with nausea. My limbs felt chilled. It was all I could manage to make the Sign of the Cross.

"No wonder you couldn't stay here, Bagha Khan," I said quietly.

But even in the midst of all this death, there was hope. The electric light flashed over gold and the kindly features of a woman's face. I scrambled through the bones towards what I had seen and shone the light full on it.

For a moment, I quite forgot why I was there. I felt overpowered by the love that was written on the Woman's face, the wisdom in the Child's. I reached out and ran my fingertips along the image then, kneeling, I kissed it reverently. I felt compelled. I couldn't do anything else.

"Lady, what can I do?" I asked in a whisper.

The Lady's eyes gazed with love upon me, as if from a vast distance but also from a very intimate closeness at the same time.

"How can I save you?" I wondered.

I blinked. Perhaps it was just a trick of the electric light held in my unsteady hand, or perhaps it was a miracle. But for a moment it had seemed that the lips of the ancient image had actually moved. "You can't," the shape of the lips said silently. "Only trust." It must have been an illusion, I thought, though I remained unconvinced.

I shrugged off my pack, unfastened the straps, and gently placed the icon inside. Then I put the pack on, waded through the bones to the rope, and began my ascent.

A few moments later, I had pulled myself back up onto the floor of the stupa.

"Ah, Herr McCracken, a mere eight minutes," said Von Krems. "Now, the icon, if you please."

My hands shook as I unclasped the backpack. I drew out the icon and held it up for my friends and family to see.

Sikorsky darted forward and threw himself to the ground before the icon, kissing it quickly before two of the soldiers grabbed him by each arm and cast him to the ground beside the others. Laughing, Von Krems seized the icon and set it against the foot of the World Tree.

Rabotnik, I saw, had a deeply troubled expression on his face. I could just see the eight-point crucifix tattooed on his neck.

Laughing, Von Krems said, "Soon, Rabotnik, you will be free of superstition for ever!" He stood back and leveled his Luger right at the face of the Lady.

Von Krems' finger squeezed the trigger.

CHAPTER 16
A MIRACULOUS SOLUTION

A deep *boom!* that was not the report of the pistol shook the stupa from the tip of the dome right down to the ghastly cavern below our feet. Thirteen pairs of eyes looked up and around. The ceiling of the stupa trembled. Chunks of plaster and masonry began to tumble from the edges of the cracks, then gaps appeared among the branches of the World Tree. I dived over to Ari and Archie and held the toddler close, shielding him from the falling rocks.

An earthquake, I thought.

But then I heard Sikorsky's voice: "McCracken, look!"

I followed his pointing finger, and saw that a shadow lay across the floor of the stupa. It reminded me a lot of the shadow cast by the farm machinery in the ramshackle barn in Switzerland, all those months ago. But looking round, I could not see anything that had cast it.

The boom had become a prolonged rumble. The walls shook and the World Tree swayed as if in a high wind. Von Krems cried out, an agonized and despairing scream.

But there was one sound: a laugh of pure merriment. To my surprise, it was Rabotnik who was laughing, out of pure delight. He dropped the cannonball and reached up to touch the tattoo on his neck.

With a mighty crack, a shaft of sunlight thrust like a piston through the gloom of the stupa as a large patch of ceiling dislodged itself and shattered against the ground. I could feel smaller pieces showering my back. The ground shook continually, as if a massive and badly oiled machine were running beneath it.

Escape!

The word suddenly occurred to me. That was our first priority: escape. Scooping Archie in one arm, I reached out to grab Ari and lead them out to the open air, where there would at least be less danger from falling masonry. But even as we stood, the entire back half of the ceiling fell onto the four Bolshevik soldiers. The shock wave threw me over backwards. Archie rolled away from me as a cloud of dust billowed outwards and over us.

"Whee!" sang Archie.

But he had rolled over next to the chasm in the floor. Ari and I both scrambled for him. He started to get to his feet, unsteadily as the floor vibrated under him.

Von Krems still stood beside the icon, his pistol in his hand, his arm outstretched rigidly. His eyes were fixed upon the ground at his feet. The shadow I had seen earlier seemed to be coming towards him, and he turned the pistol on it, letting loose one shot after another until the clip was empty and the breech block just made a series of hollow snapping noises that were completely engulfed by the roaring of the earthquake.

I reached Archie a moment before Ari and swiped him away from the edge of the fissure. As I did so, another crack appeared, like a tributary to a river. It split the stupa into three parts.

The remaining ceiling trembled still. I held Ari and Archie close, my back pelted with large falling stones. Slowly, the rocky shower subsided and I looked up.

The entire ceiling of the stupa was gone. The walls had vanished. Deep piles of rough stone lay all around. Only the World Tree still stood, Von Krems clinging to it for his life.

Chaikin took one look around at the devastation, then clearly resolved his mind. Seizing the icon from where Von Krems had set it, he leaped over the widening crack in the floor to join us. Rabotnik watched him go, a wide grin on his ugly face, then jumped after him.

I passed Archie to Ari and held out my hand. "Von Krems!" I yelled. "Jump! We can save you!"

"No one can save me!" screamed Von Krems.

"Just jump to us!" I shouted back.

"*Nein!*" He shook his head frantically. "The crack, it is too wide!"

"I'll catch you!" My foot was on the very edge of the crack, and I saw pieces of the mosaic under my toes tumbling into the darkness.

"*Die Welt endet!*" Von Krems wailed. "The world, it ends! It is not safe!"

A tremendous pulse flung the floor upwards six inches, casting us all to the ground. Von Krems screamed as the World Tree dropped suddenly through the floor and into the terrible cavern beneath.

We ran. The stupa did not exist any more, but we ran, this way and that to avoid piles of broken stone, until we were in the courtyard again.

Starting with the place where the World Tree had stood, the floor began to collapse, and the collapse rippled outwards until a circular depression, fifty feet in diameter, lay where the stupa had once stood. What was left of the walls collapsed inwards, with grinding crashes and fountaining plumes of dust. When the dust began to clear, the ground before us was almost perfectly level. At long last, all those grisly bodies had been properly buried. The little island vibrated one last time.

"Look!" It was Ari's voice. "Look at the sun!"

I raised my eyes. Through the dust, the sun was nothing but a plaque of dull silver, and I wondered for a moment what Ari could have meant me to look at. But then something else happened. The sun trembled, like a rose in a breeze. It shook in the heavens.

"Is it an eclipse?" wondered Ari.

I shook my head. I couldn't speak.

A breath of wind blew in my face. The wind grew stronger, and I was forced to my knees. The wind roared around us like a tornado. It screamed like a locomotive's whistle in a tunnel. I shielded my face with my hand, for the wind caught up smaller pieces of debris and pelted them left and right. Ari was on her knees, Archie held tightly to her. I put my arms about them both and buried my face in my family. I heard that Ari was praying the *Ave Maria*.

Slowly, the noise and the titanic wind died down, and we all looked up again.

A marvelous blue light lay all around us, which changed slowly to a golden glow. We all knelt. Rabotnik had covered his face with his hands, and his shoulders shook. Grubworthy's cheeks were wet with tears.

The golden light flowed out from the sun and onto the walls of the ancient monastery, the blue waters all around, the snow and the distant mountains. The air grew warmer around us, until it was almost tropical. The ice on the lake grew dark as it melted, and the aeroplane that had brought the communists to Por-Bazhyn dipped its nose and slid beneath the waters.

The sun seemed to go out and light up again. But now it was in a different place. It flickered, it danced. Slowly at first, it began to rotate, sending out beams of light in all directions. It looked like a firework I used to love as a boy, called a Catherine Wheel. It spun and sparked, rays flashing from it as it turned.

I don't know how long this went on. To us, it seemed over soon, but when we looked back on it, it seemed also to have lasted for ever. But spinning, the sun eventually started to drift like a flaming petal towards the horizon. In the end, it sank behind the distant mountains in a blaze of fire, and instantly the stars shone with a bold light, as if singing of glory.

Slowly, we came to ourselves. I got to my feet, helping Ari and Archie up after me. We had no words as we gathered, but my eyes and Fritz's met. We did not know what we had seen, but we knew we both had seen it. Sikorsky dusted himself off without any words.

Grubworthy blinked, pushed himself to his feet, and looked at us with a sheepish smile. He wiped his cheeks dry with the back of his hand.

Rabotnik had not moved. I touched him on the shoulder, and he looked up. There were things like scales on his eyes, and he evidently could see nothing. I helped him to his feet, and Chaikin stepped forward to provide an arm for his support.

Still we had not spoken. Words seemed inadequate. We picked our way through the ruins to the lake, which was now water, not ice. There, we sat down and faced one another, sitting in a circle of friends. Even Rabotnik.

Eventually, Sikorsky got to his feet. "I will bring LS3," he said, and waded into the lake. Fritz got up and followed him. For a few moments we could see their heads, picked out by the brilliant starlight, as they swam to the far side. At a soft little grunt, I turned my head, to see Archie asleep in his mother's arms.

Some minutes after this, we heard the engines start up—all four of them. I smiled. The engines were no longer frozen.

Moments later, the dark shape of the LS3 blotted out the stars above our head with its vast cigar-shape. A square of light shone from the gondola's hatch, and the rope ladder tumbled down towards us. One by one, we ascended. Ari came last, handing Archie up to me before climbing the ladder and entering the gondola.

Fritz had put out some bread and cold meats in the dining room, and we all found that we possessed hearty appetites. The clock behind the bar told me that it was a little after ten o'clock.

Chaikin had rested the icon of Our Lady of Kazan against the stern wall, and from there she watched us with deep love. She was completely un-damaged.

Grubworthy swallowed. He had not, I noticed, eaten with the rest of us. Catching my eye, he said, "I saw her."

"The Lady of Kazan?"

"The lady—the lady in blue. At first, I thought she was the Welsh princess from the play I saw. But no. It was her." He waved a finger in the general direction of the icon. "She held the child."

Ari caught her breath. "Did she say anything?"

"Oh yes." Grubworthy broke into a wide smile. "Oh yes, she did." But that was all he would ever say on the subject.

We left Chaikin and the blind Rabotnik in Kungurtuk, at the cabin of an English missionary named Higgins. He had not seen the sun dance as we all had. Not that we spoke of it to him—it seemed somehow too solemn to mention in casual conversation. But he was a chatty old mannie, and would surely have mentioned it if he had seen anything like it. That made us wonder, as the LS3 left Tuva and Kungurtuk and Por-Bazhyn behind, exactly what it was we had seen.

Sikorsky calculated we had enough fuel to reach Delhi in northern India. There, we were able to re-fuel, crossing the Indian subcontinent and flying over the Indian Ocean. Up we went between Arabia and Africa, and then out into the Mediterranean.

199

From there, we flew through the Straits of Gibraltar and around the Iberian Peninsula and came at last to the coast of England early in December. The sky was grey as we watched the green fields float by under us, and rain lashed against the forward windows, beading and running in silver lines to left and right.

It was difficult to fly a zeppelin over Britain during the War, and we had our encounters with fighters of the Royal Flying Corps. But they did not open fire when we draped a Union Jack from the gondola. They did, however, escort us to the RFC aerodrome at Andover, Hampshire, where we were obliged to explain ourselves to the commanding officer. He, being at length satisfied by our story, cabled London, and we experienced no further interference until we landed at RFC Rochford where, through the grey rain, we could just make out the Thames Estuary.

Sikorsky shut off the engines, and the kind of stillness settled over the LS3 that always seems to come at the end of an adventure. We looked at one another in a kind of bemused foolishness, uncertain what to say to conclude things. Ari was eating ice-cream and a steak, which she had just requested from Fritz.

We were all startled by a rapping sound from the passageway and, after a moment, we realized that someone had knocked on the hatch. Fritz hurried away and returned a moment later accompanied by an officer of the Royal Flying Corps who introduced himself as Major Pretyman.

"You must forgive my curiosity, gentlemen and lady," he said. "I am the commanding officer of Number 61 Squadron, and our task is to defend London against zeppelins. I was as pleased as punch to find a friendly zeppelin would be visiting us at Rochford."

"Have you bagged one yet?" I asked.

"Not yet," admitted the major. "Got a Gotha a few days ago, but one of our fellows had a bit of an accident with a flare pistol and the whole blasted thing went up in flames." He looked about himself in awe, marveling at the bar, the tables and chairs, the wide windows. "I must say, this is a sight pleasanter than the insides of most zeppelins— according to what I've read and the pictures I've seen, that is."

"If you would like tour, I would be glad to show you round," said Sikorsky, rising from his seat and pleased, as always, to show off.

"I say, that would be most awfully nice of you, Mr. Sikorsky. Oh, by the way." He fished in his breast pocket and produced a small yellow envelope. "Cable for you, Mr. McCracken."

"Thanks." As Pretyman exited talking excitedly to Sikorsky, I ripped open the telegram. "It's from Fr. Jamie." The priest had accompanied me on several adventures, and was one of the men I most admired in the world. "He's in Portugal again. He says, 'Come soon. Miraculous.' That's all."

"I'd like to stay put for a while," commented Ari. "And before we go gallivanting off again, we have to find a place for the icon."

"I can take it with me," volunteered Grubworthy.

"Of course you can, Cadwallader."

"You're still sure, then?" I asked. Grubworthy nodded. I looked out of the window. The sky was the colour of iron. "Fritz, you'd better put the canopy up on the Daimler."

Two hours later, the Daimler was chugging along through Knightsbridge. The crowds on the pavements seemed very oddly dressed to me, and I realized that they were just normal English men and women. There were young men in boaters, ladies in long skirts, soldiers and sailors on leave—there were even American soldiers in their strange boy-scout hats, for America had entered the War while we were on our adventure—a little glimmer of hope in those dark years, with communism triumphant not so very far away. Fritz applied the brakes and we rolled to a stop in front of Brompton Oratory, that magnificent structure of marble that looks a couple of hundred years old, but had actually been built only thirty years previously.

"Here we are, Cadwallader," said Ari brightly.

"Thank you for everything," said Grubworthy. "You've made a very great difference in my life. I shall think of you always. And you shall . . . you shall always be in my prayers."

I gave him a big smile. "Well, that's going to be your main business from now on."

As he stepped down from the motor-car, it rocked, and I thought the suspension gave a little sigh of relief. Reaching into the vehicle, he took the icon, which was wrapped in brown paper, and tucked it under his arm. After a moment, he disappeared through the door of the Oratory and was gone.

"Can you take us to Regent Street, please, Fritz?" said Ari.

"What's there?" I asked.

"A department store I want to visit."

Fritz put the car in gear and we motored off. As we passed Hyde Park, where American soldiers were parading, I mused, "Odd to think of old Grubworthy in a monk's habit, isn't it? He'll look just like Friar Tuck."

Ari gave a smile and a nod. "He's already lost a lot of weight."

"Yeah, he must be down to about 330 pounds. Are you all right?"

"I'm just feeling a bit queasy this morning, that's all."

"Fritz, can you slow down a little?" I asked, leaning forward. "Mrs. McCracken is feeling some motion sickness."

"She is *not*, Herr McCracken."

"What?" I was taken aback by Fritz's tone, but before I could say anything by way of reprimand, Ari spoke.

"Stop here, please, Fritz."

The shop outside which we stopped sold toys and other children's items and sported bright red awnings. "Hamley's," I said. "Are we buying somethign for Archie?" A terrible thought struck me. "Have I missed his birthday?"

"That's not until next month, dear." Ari opened the door and stepped down onto the pavement. Pushing on the brass handle of the door, we entered the warm interior together.

"I don't get it," I said. "What are we here for?"

"New baby supplies," answered Ari. "We left all the newborn stuff in the Honduras."

"New baby?"

Ari smiled and tugged my arm. "Come on," she said, "I'll buy you a baby stroller."

THE END

FROM FRITZ'S KITCHEN

Pelmeni

Ingredients

2 c. flour	½ lb. ground beef
1 c. milk or water	½ lb. ground pork
½ tsp. salt	1 onion, chopped fine
1 tbs. vegetable oil	Salt and pepper
3 eggs	Sour cream or butter

1. **Directions**
    Combine beef and pork and add onion, salt, and pepper.
2. Mix flour with eggs and milk, salt to taste and oil until a soft dough forms. Knead on floured surface until dough is elastic.
3. Take some dough and roll it to make a sausage shape about one inch in diameter. Divide into pieces (1 inch thick. Roll each piece so that it is very thin, about 1/16 inch thick.
4. Cut the dough out in rounds about 2 inches in diameter. Fill each round with 1 tbs. of the mincemeat and fold into half-circles and crimp the edge to seal.

5. Bring together the corners of the half-circles and pinch them together.
6. Boil a large amount of salted water, as they can stick together. Carefully drop pelmeni into boiling water. Don't forget to stir them from time to time. Boil for 20 minutes.
7. Serve with butter or sour cream.

Georgian Salad

Ingredients
2 cucumbers
1 onion, sliced
4 diced tomatoes
2 tbs. red wine vinegar
Fresh coriander, basil, flat-leaf parsley and dill
salt and black pepper to taste

Directions
Combine all ingredients, mix well and chill thoroughly.

 Like the famous Cat, Mark Adderley was born in Cheshire, England. His early influences included C. S. Lewis and adventure books of various kinds, and his teacher once wrote on his report card, "He should go in for being an author," advice that stuck with him. He studied for some years at the University of Wales, where he became interested in medieval literature, particularly the legend of King Arthur. But it was in graduate school that he met a clever and beautiful American woman, whom he moved to the United States to marry. He spent some time as a professor of literature, and is now the director of the Via Nova Catholic Education Program and a baker for Loafers Bakery in Yankton, South Dakota. He is the author of a number of novels about King Arthur for adults, and originally wrote the McCracken books for his younger two children.

Made in the USA
Middletown, DE
22 December 2021

56884709R00119